An Anthony Rogue Novel

A LUCKY MAN

PETE ROGAN

Rogue Agent

This book is dedicated to my wife, who was my inspiration for picking up this story and getting it written. She supports my work and is the love of my life.

The book is dedicated to my kids who are the center of my world, and being storytellers themselves, both inspire me to share these stories for others to read.

It is dedicated to my dad who told me years ago he thought I was secretly a spy, giving life to the storyline for this book.

Finally, this story would not be in your hands without the support and encouragement of a great friend. Jeff - thank you for kicking my butt into action.

Contents

Chapter One

ACCIDENT IN ARVADA

Impact. A sensation of spinning. Everything went blank. When would it stop? Then, suddenly, with a thud, a halt to the spinning and movement. Something hit my shoulder. I opened my eyes. Was I OK? Yeah, I think so. What about Ray…and Elaine. They were in the front seat. I looked over the seat and saw them both, moving I think. Ray had something all over him, something red or brown. It looked too runny to be blood. Was it blood? Oh my God, was he ok?

Elaine spoke up, "I'm OK. Ray, Anthony, how about you?"

I said, "Yeah, I'm OK."

What had just happened. An accident obviously, but what happened and how? Did Ray answer? Ray?

Ray is my brother. Elaine is his wife - at the time she was his new wife of almost a year. I have three brothers, but Ray is the one I am closest to in age, and closest to in our relationship. He's 3 years older than me. We have a good bond that somehow has seemed to get stronger over the years just as the physical distance between us grew and we lived in different cities, states, or countries.

Ray and I had always shared a bedroom when we were young. When my family moved to Texas just before I started high school, Ray and I stopped sharing a bedroom. Our brother Henry stayed in Indiana for high school, then moved off to college in the midwest. And our sister Kath, the oldest of the whole family, had essentially moved out a few years before when she headed off to college in Chicago. Our brother Mike, just a year younger than Kath, had his own room after going to school in California, then coming home for a few years to get his career in golf started. So, in Texas, Ray and I were able to have our own rooms too. Somehow, not having to share that space allowed us the choice of spending time together, which led us to getting closer as friends. Mike and I also built a friendship on top of being brothers, but that came later, after we both had left home for good.

I've looked up to Ray all my life. While close in age to me, Ray was old enough to have more maturity and experience than me. He was someone to come to for advice on girls, someone who influenced my taste in music, someone who got to buy a guitar or pierce his ear long before I'd have a chance to do such a thing. In our family, Henry had pierced his ear first. Yet, when Ray got his ear pierced, it made the idea cool to me. There was something about how Ray and I overlapped in interests and world view that allowed a friendship to build. I wanted to follow in his footsteps. I lived vicariously through him. I wanted to get along with his friends.

So, being in the middle of a car accident, not knowing about his condition was stressful.

Many of my earliest memories involve Ray in some way. When I was 4, days away from turning 5, I joined a local football team. I remember going to get my equipment the first week and trying it on. I got to dress up just like my older brothers, just like Ray and Henry and Mike. I ended up not liking football, running away from practice, refusing to go on the field during games. But, that first night, I wanted to be like the big boys who played. So, I put on my pads over my clothes and put on my helmet. Then, I thought it would be fun to try on Ray's helmet. But, I couldn't get it on – it was too small. Ray tried my helmet and it was all big and wobbly on him. I was almost five, he was eight, but my head was one helmet size bigger than his. Realizing that weird disconnect between our ages and our body sizes that day has always remained with me.

Just a year before this car accident, Ray and I got another chance to grow in our brotherly friendship. I came back from living in Europe after college and had some down time. After a few weeks living at home with my folks, I got sent to Arvada, Colorado for an Agency project. Arvada, a suburb near Denver, was where Ray was living. Heck, I moved into his house a few months before he married Elaine – literally the weekend they moved into a place together - I was basically horning in on their newlywed months. I was lucky to get to re-connect with Ray, and also to get to know Elaine, who clearly is someone special to my brother.

Now, we were in the car together, wrapping up my year in Colorado with them by taking a road trip. I was heading to Utah for a new assignment from the Agency. Elaine has a sister in Utah, so Ray and Elaine were going to visit Elaine's sister. We chose to drive together instead of all hopping on planes.

That morning, we were leaving the neighborhood where Ray and Elaine's condo was, heading out a back way I rarely traveled. We came down a hill toward a light, solidly green, not ready to turn yellow and having not been red for quite a while. Down the hill lay a major thoroughfare, with a central median and two lanes in each direction. We slowed down at the bottom of the hill, started through the intersection, then …

That impact. Such a surprise. It made absolutely no sense.

So, here I was, apparently mostly OK, Elaine talking to me, and Ray with some liquid all over him. But, from Ray, no response yet. And the image in my mind was something red all over him - brown, red, I'm not sure. I immediately got concerned that something major had happened to my brother. It was hard to envision what it would be like to lose him. I have been fortunate to have few people really close to me fall ill or die. My grandmother passed away when I was 10, and my grandpa on the other side of the family when I was a teenager, but that was half a lifetime away. And everyone I cared about had been healthy and safe since then. Things in the Agency were more volatile, but in my personal life, little loss to speak of. To lose my big brother Ray - to lose any of my older siblings - would have left an amazing hole in my life. The prospect stunned me.

When accidents like this happen, it's always the driver who is hurt the worst. You hear things on the news like, "The driver was killed on impact, but his passengers have been released from the hospital tonight." That impact. That surprising, sudden impact was what could take someone away in an instant. It seemed like such a long time with no response from Ray. But, I bet it was only 2 or 3 seconds. And he did finally respond.

"I'm OK, too." Ray said, "This stuff on me. It's my coffee, it's not blood. At least I think so..."

Good, wow. It wasn't blood. We were all OK, it seemed.

So then, what the heck happened?

There we were, in the white sedan, sitting at a green light, with the left side of our car up against the curb, facing the opposite direction of traffic. How did we get pushed straight to the side, from our lane to the oncoming lane? I don't get it.

I remember spinning around. But, if we spun around, did we just stay in one spot, no longer moving forward and simply spinning to the side.

Wait, as I looked out ahead, beyond coffee-covered Ray, beyond Elaine, across the street. That's not where we were headed. That's where we came from.

We had gone out into the intersection and spun around and around, ending up on the opposite side of this main thoroughfare, looking back at where we had come down the hill. How did we make it across the intersection without hitting someone or something else? What did we hit in that impact? Where did we get hit? So many questions rushed through my head.

We got out of the car, carefully to kind of connect and check on each other. The training kicked in, and I was totally focused on figuring out what happened, what was up with our car and what state the three of us were in. Quickly, Ray, I think, popped his attention to the other car. There must've been another car. But, where? Who? Were they alright? Ray found them up on the grass about 100 yards down the road from us. Wow! How did that happen? Who knows, but Ray's concern was for their safety. Maybe it was Elaine that brought this up first – I don't recall, but it wasn't me. So, Ray walked over and checked on them while Elaine and I tried to work out what had happened.

This is how it seems to have occurred. We came down the hill, rolling into the intersection, slowing down because of the hill going into a green light. The car that hit us was on their way somewhere important – not like a mother in labor was in the back, but something urgent was on their mind. They came zooming down this main thoroughfare going 50 mph or so, faster than the limit. They totally missed the red light in front of them and started sailing through it.

As we came down the hill, they passed just in front of us. Ray remembers a bit of a flash of something, but no clear picture of a car passing before him. Just enough to prompt him to try to hit the brakes. So, they didn't hit us as much as we hit them. It wasn't our fault, there was no time to avoid the collision, and we had the clear right of way coming through our green light. Yet, the timing was such that we hit them. The damage to our car was on the front bumper along the left.

The force of the impact ended up rotating our car. Their forward momentum pulled the front of our car perpendicular to our original movement, spinning our car around like a top. It's hard to say how many rotations we did – maybe just ½ a spin, maybe more – before coming to rest up against the curb on that far side of the intersection.

It was lucky for Ray and I that they passed in front of us. Had we been just a second or two ahead of where we were, the other car would've broadsided the driver side, where he and I were both sitting. There would've been a good chance that one or both of us would not have survived. And, because we were slowing down for the intersection at the bottom of the hill, we actually did not hit their car all that hard.

This accident was the first of a season of near misses for me. This one almost de-railed the project in Utah altogether, before it had even begun. Had my brother Ray been more aggressive in getting to the bottom of that hill, or had the other driver been going 1 mph slower, the impact would've crushed our side of the car. To have such an unexpected, surprising accident occur - to be able to have all of us walk away with nothing more than a sore shoulder - it was amazing. To be so close to losing my big brother - it was an eye opener. I was young enough to still feel fairly invincible. But, this took a hit out of that confidence. It reminded such a young man how fragile life is and how quickly it can be taken away.

Chapter Two

AFTER ARVADA

"Hello. Yes, I am OK. I think I am OK. Wow! That was a doozy," he said, shaking his head a bit.

Schelletz expected to feel an impact, but something had gone wrong. Where was the other car? The man who approached Schelletz was pointing over to the other car, smiling. There was genuine concern in his eyes. He was just another person on the road, unfortunate enough to be dealing with this accident.

Schelletz wanted nothing more than to pull his car back on the road and get out of there. He didn't want to be talking to this guy. Or to anyone.

"My name is Ray. I've called the police. They are on their way, along with an ambulance. I think you should stay in the car until they get here. You landed in a safe spot, away from traffic."

Yep, there it was. Next, it would be the police and paramedics. Oh, how could he explain that one?

"Great! Thanks. You can call me Schelletz. I'll just sit here and wait. Are you sure the car is in a safe spot?"

Ray looked around then walked around Schelletz's car to help out and make sure he was safe.

This was meant to be demolition derby, not an episode of E.R. His mission was to strike their car, hard. Hard enough to kill Anthony Rogue. Maybe the others would suffer the same fate, but Anthony Rogue would be dead - that was their clear directive, to get rid of Anthony Rogue. It wasn't for Schelletz to ask why - it was just for him to do, to accomplish the directive. Clearly, as Rogue stood by the side of the road, looking over the car, he was not dead. But would he know what was really happening? Would he suspect and come over to deal with Schelletz directly?

No, not in front of his family. Those in the Agency still lived as if family was off limits. Rogue should know better than that. The Oligarchs were not concerned about who else was caught in the crossfire. They just wanted Rogue dead, as long as Schelletz made it look like an accident.

Well, he gave them an accident. But, not the one they'd expected. Looking at Rogue's car, and his own, he knew what happened. His timing was off, entering the intersection before them. They had struck him, but he was trying to time it so he'd crush their car on the driver's side. Damn, the timing device had failed him. "Wait," Schelletz thought, "Could this Ray guy see the device?" He looked down - it had shut off on impact. It looked just like a car GPS, so the guy wouldn't know what it was.

"Your car is safe. No liquids leaking. Far enough up on this curb that no traffic will come by."

"OK. Thanks again. I am OK. You should go back to your family." Schelletz needed to get rid of the guy so he could call the Oligarchs. It would not be a pleasant call, but they should hear about this from him, not from someone else.

Chapter Three

GETTING TO UTAH

I was glad we came out of the accident in good shape. We were all stiff and sore, but the paramedics had confirmed there were no internal injuries. While I had pain in my shoulder, my brother and his wife were doing quite well. They were shaken up, but if they had injuries, they weren't showing up right away.

Well then, their car was not going anywhere. Certainly not to Salt Lake City. Ray and Elaine quickly cancelled their plans. A long weekend with Elaine's sister would have been fun, but now they had a car to attend to, expenses to deal with, and no inclination to buy plane tickets, hop on a jet, and suddenly be 500 miles from home.

I had more at stake, though. I was supposed to meet up with Hal at the university the next day. The Navajo Project was a go. I needed to be in Monument Valley by the end of the week. Since I had nothing tying me to Arvada, Ray understood my desire to follow through with the summer in Utah. The cover story I had about teaching programming to Navajo youth was compelling - the Agency was good with cover stories. Ray and Elaine were really supportive, helping me turn around quickly to get on a plane.

I liked how the Agency kept a normal life in hand for me, for all of us. I suppose you could call it deep cover, but in some ways it was more than that. It was almost like the witness relocation program. You lived an everyday life - no one knew the real work you did. I never had to change my identity, take a different name, use a fake passport, wear a disguise or a silly Mission Impossible mask. Heck, few people in the world knew our part of the Agency even existed. In extreme cases, some of us had to assume a different identity, but that was thankfully rare.

With the temporary loan, off I flew, flight 213 from DIA to SLC. Hal and Bill met me at the airport. I'd never been to Salt Lake City. I drove through southern Utah with my buddies back in the day, but we totally avoided Salt Lake.

The city was not quite what I'd expected. Hearing about the conservative Mormon lifestyle, you expect kind of a small town feel - almost dirt roads and wagons. But, Salt Lake had expressways, large supermarkets, national restaurant chains, movie theaters, even liquor stores. It was a clean, modern American city. Nestled up against the Rocky Mountains, with minimal pollution and blue skies, a small downtown and modestly average building heights, it seemed quite idyllic. Hal could tell all kinds of stories about how stifling the local culture was for non-Mormons like himself, but that was more subtle than what I would experience in those 2 days of mission briefing.

Bill was a housemate who had been 2 years behind me at Caltech. So, when I learned he and his dad would train me in on the Navajo Project, I was both surprised and relieved. Surprised that my college buddy had also been recruited by the Agency. Relieved that I was working with someone I knew and trusted. As much as you know and trust anyone within the Agency. After all, we were all trained to hide our true work.

Still, we had our instant rapport, enjoying the weekend to catch up, as well as train in. It seemed Bill would be there in Monument Valley as an instructor too. Hal had been running the program for years - a genuine outreach project from the university to the tribal community. Hal had connected with a Native American educator who had conceptualized this bridge between the cultures, a bridge from programming to math, to geometry and patterns of weaving, all the way back to the ancient crafts of the indigenous peoples. Hal's educator friend had started with Inuit tribes of the arctic where she was from. Hal had adapted it to the Diné of the Four Corners. They called it the Bridges Program.

A year or two into the Bridges Program, Hal started noticing patterns in the profile of the program's most successful kids. It was not just an accident that they all expressed the same 5 traits. Hal put two and two together and realized the unique visual and linguistic skills of these kids had a potential application. So, he contacted a linguistics professor in Monterey, CA named van Gotsche and his old buddies at the Agency. Van Gotsche put together and pitched a plan.

These kids were the descendants of the Codetalkers. In World War II, the government needed a code that was effective, but impenetrable by the Japanese, who were master code breakers, always listening to US transmissions. It was ingenious in its simplicity. To encode a message from two American outposts in the war, one commander would provide the message to a Codetalker - a trained Navajo youth. The Codetalker would deliver the message over open channels. On the other end, another Talker would get the message and unpack it for the local commander. The "code" was essentially a simple Navajo translation of the original English. Over time, sure, they developed another layer of specialized language - to obscure the message further. It may or may not have been necessary. Records recovered after the war showed the effort the Japanese went through to crack the code. They had hours of recorded messages. They spent thousands of man hours trying to decode and interpret it. All in vain. Never any closer to understanding the messages than when they started. They had no linguistic knowledge of the speech patterns of the Navajo, so the key was ever elusive.

The Navajo Project was not about encoding messages, but it was going to leverage the same linguistic gifts of the tribe. These kids had been brought up between cultures - one leg in Navajo culture, speaking the language with their grandparents, living miles away from each other in the disperse, nomadic traditions of their nation. One leg in US culture, watching episodes of Friends, cheering for the Utah Jazz each winter, going to a high school that looked on the outside like any other public school in the country. The ones who stood out in the Bridges Program had thread that needle perfectly.

Their roots were on the reservation, so the class had to be in their high school. They quickly mastered the traditional techniques of rug weaving, basket making, and bead work, showing both their ties to their culture, but also their mental agility in recognizing and holding patterns in their minds. The programming lessons took hold quickly - their math skills and logic flowed well with the visual design projects to create on-screen maps of the weaving and bead designs they were developing on the looms in the other room. Sending that cursor line by line across the screen to develop the complex designs of their elders was a revelation to them. They understood the power of recursion and code structures to efficiently represent that ancient wisdom in the most modern of forms. These kids were living bridges from Monument Valley to Silicon Valley.

It was my job to take that raw talent, point it in the right direction and show them how they could bridge themselves beyond Silicon Valley and into the global community. They could serve the Navajo nation, the United States, and the efforts for peace and stability around the world all at once. But, first, I had to find them and meet them.

————————

"I'm nervous about this, Anthony," said Hal. He paused.

I considered jumping in. A hundred questions popped to mind. But, I waited instead.

"I've spent so many years building this program, building relationships. The community has deep trust in me now. I'm worried this project will destroy the things I've worked so hard to build, the accomplishments so many others have built."

"Hal, this will not destroy any of that," I responded. "It will strengthen your role and relationships. This project provides a clear path forward for the brightest of these kids. What draws them into the program will be their rich understanding of where they come from. What makes them the right kids will be their talents in this new area of programming, which the community will see as a new avenue for development of their children. You are not betraying anything or anyone; you are taking the next step in evolving the program."

"That sounds so nice when you say it, but..." Hal trailed off.

"Hal, don't forget. This was your idea. You were the brilliant mind that saw the possibilities here. I am simply your agent, helping bring that idea to life. We'll be building this bridge together." I smiled as I bared my feelings about the importance of this project.

That was the end of the conversation. Hal moved forward from then on. Every now and then, a hesitation would appear in his actions or words. But, then a smile would spread, his shoulders would relax, and he'd ease back into the task at hand.

After a few days of organizing, discussing, and writing up materials, we were ready. It was time to make our way to Monument Valley.

I had seen photographs of the valley. Iconic buttes - deep red hues - stark, unforgiving vistas - natural beauty, uninterrupted by the scars of human life. But, those were two dimensional representations. Even in the Mexican restaurant commercials, with panning and zooming, the images were still primarily flat. Driving there would bring it to life. The scenery would change from urban foothills like Salt Lake, to suburban sprawl like Provo, to rural small town like Moab. The highlights shifted from stark Rocky Mountain vistas to bland, open expanses, shifting to cliffs and muted buttes around Moab. Then, the open desert took hold for miles on end. I began to wonder when we'd ever get there.

The highway finally led to a cliff side, with a drop off well below. It could've been the setting for the final scene in Thelma and Louise. But the road took a turn and started a switchback down the cliff. Looking out toward the horizon, there was a wide open, flat landscape stretching as far forward as you could see. But it lay 1000 feet below the road we were on. It was as if we were dropping down into a large lake, or into the sea, just with no water below.

I could see one house, maybe a mile away from the bottom of the cliff, with absolutely nothing around it. Bill mentioned that it was a B & B - clearly specializing in a remote, roughing-it style experience. Visibility was awesome, as the view stretched out for miles across this valley floor, with no clouds, no pollution, no hills obscuring the open expanse. Way in the distance, some outcroppings could be seen, but the details were unclear. I felt at once suddenly close to our destination - like I knew we had entered the neighborhood - but I also felt a long way from the destination; I could see so far in front of us and there was clearly nothing worth stopping at. After another twenty minutes, we pulled into a quiet, modest and dusty town. There was a trading post here. We stopped, filled up on gas, used the restroom, and stocked up on snacks.

"So, where are we?" I asked.

"Mexican Hat, it's called," said Hal. "But, more importantly, we are only about 15 minutes from the high school. This is the closest town. There's nothing but rock formations and the occasional isolated home between us and the school."

"Well, let's get it done!" I said. And off we went.

Turning south along Highway 163 from the western edge of Mexican Hat, the red rocks finally started punctuating the scenery. They were gorgeous. Each one clearly like the others, but still as unique as a fingerprint. The road was winding back and forth, up and down, around bends, then straight at one of the buttes. We'd get to see it up close - the scale, the texture, the detail to the layers of rock. The rough rock face looked like someone had just chiseled it from a larger formation. It seemed fresh and young, yet it had been there for decades, centuries. The wind constantly polished it, giving it that clean, crisp finish. Along the bottom was a mound of sand on all sides. It was as if a giant toddler was at the beach, pushing these rocks into the sand, then piling little mounds up around all sides to help "plant" the rock in place. But, no toddler had ever carried these rocks anywhere. The mounds of sand were evidence of the ever-changing landscape that one day would wear these down to bumps in the desert, losing their stark beauty. We are so lucky to live at a time when we can see them, visit the valley, and approach them up close. They are true works of art, thousands of years in the making.

The detail was amazing. From a distance, you'd see one outline. As you got closer, the bumps and notches along the edge would zoom in and sharpen, revealing a new layer of detail - bumps and notches that made up each of the large bumps. Then, as we got closer, the next layer of detail would become obvious, showing even more subtle variations in shape. It seemed infinitely endless, like you could walk right up to it, revealing another two or three layers of detail. Then, you could shrink yourself down to the size of an ant and see two more layers of close up detail. Did it ever stop?

We zipped by that first, dramatic, long butte. There were dozens dotting the landscape in all directions. It felt like we had suddenly entered a moonscape or an alien world. The openness, the shape of the road, and the dramatic landmarks of the formations which inspired drivers to pour on the speed. Something about the scene just called out for speed, and Hal complied, modestly, but nonetheless, moving at a brisk pace through this aptly named Monument Valley.

The rock formations did give the impression of monuments - carved deliberately to memorialize long forgotten heroes. But what heroes? Heroes of an alien race, reinforcing the feeling of being dropped on an alien planet. Heroes of an ancient civilization and these were the ruins of monuments built 1000 years ago. They just felt so deliberate, like a planned garden, not haphazard results of millennia of mundane natural forces like water and wind.

Would Anthony Rogue ever be memorialized? Was I a hero? I'd done some important things for community and country, but were they worthy of a monument? And would anyone ever get to know the stories, or would they always be in a vault in the Agency? Stored in self-destructing cases to preserve the innocence of our great nation. Well, the kids we were recruiting for this project - they would be heroes. Hal and I would make sure of that.

Hal looked at me like he knew my thoughts. Maybe he had followed a similar line of thinking in this inspiring landscape.

"Hal, let's go find us some heroes!" We both smiled.

Chapter Four

GOING TO SCHOOL

We continued through the valley, passing dramatic buttes along the way. One was really familiar, looking like the head of a Native American with a feather sticking up from his forehead. Then, off in the distance I saw the two famous mittens, looking like giant stone hands sticking out of the earth.

We approached an intersection with a stop sign, the first one we had seen since leaving Mexican Hat. At the intersection, on the right, was a bright green grassy field with a running track around it. This was the school football field. Just behind the grassy field sat a concrete and brick high school built circa 1985. It looked like it could be a high school in any suburb in America. But, this was no suburb. No tidy neighborhood of roads and cul de sacs lined with cookie cutter homes. Just wide open desert on all sides.

Turning left at that intersection did lead up a modest hill toward Monument Valley park, the tribe-run preserve that looked after this delicate and alluring landscape, making sure it was accessible, yet maintained for future generations. That's where you could go to take a hiking tour to see the mittens and other grand vistas in the valley.

Beyond the school, perhaps a mile or so, sat two other buildings. One was a small trading post with a private campground attached - a place for people to stopover for the night if they were touring the area. Then, down a modest side street was a small medical facility run by the Seventh Day Adventists. An odd outcropping in this barren land, especially given the Mormon hold on Utah society. But, there it was nonetheless. At least if medical attention was needed, I knew where to go.

We pulled into the parking lot of the school. On one side was the entrance to the school itself. On the other was a collection of 6 modest homes. Hal explained these houses were made available as apartments for teachers who took on jobs at the high school. Many of the teachers were white folks from larger towns in Utah or Arizona. Some lived in nearby towns like Mexican Hat, but others needed housing to make the job a viable choice. So, the district had built housing.

While the school was on Navajo controlled lands, the tribe had arranged years ago for the state of Utah to run the school system as a part of the rural school district in that corner of the state. This left the school run by White people, and created a potential for lingering conflict and resentment between the tribe and the White Utah residents. Were they supporting the Navajo needs for their kids' educations? Or were they modern day colonists trying to pull the kids into US society, or evangelists trying to convert the kids to the Mormon faith?

"Jesse Squire, the current principal, has walked the line quite well for 10 years," said Hal. "She has staffed out the school with many young Navajo teachers. They attend tribal or community colleges nearby, then go off to Flagstaff to finish out the coursework needed for an education degree."

"What's the story with Squire?" I asked.

"I met her a few years ago, as we were looking to start up the Bridges Program. This is the only Navajo high school within the boundaries of Utah, so it was really our only option to start up the program. Luckily, Squire jumped at the chance to get programming in the schools. She saw the value immediately. And the tie-in to Navajo culture was a huge selling point for her."

"Does she come off as a colonist?" I asked.

"Being a non-Mormon living in Utah, I've learned to be suspicious of even people with the best of intentions. But, of all the people, Mormon or not, I've worked with in Utah, she has been the most genuinely supportive of community needs and goals, regardless of religion or culture."

At this point, we parked our dust-covered car in the mostly deserted parking lot. The only other car was a 10-year-old, dirt brown basic Japanese sedan with California plates. As we got out of the car, a door opened on a mobile classroom building at the edge of the parking lot. Out walked Steve Shimizu, another Caltech classmate.

"Steve! I had no idea you'd be here!?"

"When Bill told me what his dad was up to, you couldn't keep me away. My math degree was burning a hole in my pocket. I knew I had to dive into something real and concrete as soon as I could. Then he told me you'd be on the team and I almost pulled out." He paused, then smiled real big. "C'mon Rogue! How the heck are you?"

I laughed. "Better than you're gonna be after a week working with me."

We caught up on life and the Bridges Program over a good meal in the house we were gonna share. The team was fired up.

The next day we met with Dr. Squire to set the stage. She introduced Bill and me to the elder instructors. These women were the heart of Bridges. Without their skills and deep Navajo knowledge, we'd have no program. They all glowed with pride and energy. To be in this school, as honored instructors showed a sense of trust they had rarely felt from White people. They also understood the opportunity they had to spend time with these youngsters before they fell completely into US culture. The whole enterprise had an air of the sacred. Had there been no Agency agenda, I'd still enjoy every moment of my time there.

Hal left a few days later, and Bill, Steve, and I stepped up to run the programming side of the show. Steve had met a lot of the local residents and had many insights for me. I listened, observed, and followed his lead. The middle generation, parents of the high school kids and children of the elders, all kept a mild distance from me. They were wary enough to sense I had multiple agendas. I wasn't going to let that slow me down.

The kids ranged from age 10 to 18. Some seemed jaded at first, like their parents made them come. Soon, the elders had melted that crust and exposed them all as genuinely interested in all parts of the program. The kids learned rug weaving, basket making, or bead work in the morning. Their focus was intense. The elders led the classes, speaking only in the language of the Diné. Some of the kids were not fluent in their community's native language, but they understood all they needed to.

I joined in with a rug weaving class, fascinated by this craft that I'd seen provide a format for deep traditional storytelling in the mountain communities of Poland. I was learning the basics alongside the kids, practicing the moves to wrap yarn around the loom strands. I did not have a project of my own, but instead helped students when they were stuck. I watched the elders move quickly through elaborate and beautiful patterns on their own looms while they taught the class. It was an amazing skill to watch, and a remarkable event to witness the growth of these kids in a few days' time. I helped keep the kids in line and focused. But, I soon learned the elders had their own quiet ways of drawing the kids in, keeping them engaged, and pulling them back from distractions.

In the afternoon, Bill, Steve, and I were in the lead. We brought the kids into a computer lab, teaching them the basics of drawing using LOGO. While it is a simple language, it was well suited for introductory coding. These kids got to see how simple commands could move the turtle cursor and control the output on screen. They learned about recursion and functions. They learned logic and skills to translate visual thinking into technological design. Their end project was to reproduce the geometric pattern of their traditional craft (rug, basket, or beadwork) on-screen, using programming techniques.

The Bridges Program showed these kids how their elders carried math concepts and instruction to younger generations using these crafts. The kids strengthened their math skills through work with the elders. Then they applied that math in the computer lab. Finally, they saw how the two worlds were linked - rug weaving and coding, baskets and technology, beadwork and visual design. What an awakening.

I met Jason in the rug weaving class. He was quiet, shy on the surface, seeming a bit distant. I didn't realize it at first, but this was part of a well-cultivated Navajo trait of being a good listener. While he seemed disengaged on the surface, it became clear within a few days that he was very engaged - at such a deep level that he couldn't be bothered with the niceties of chit chat and feeding my own internal concerns about being accepted. Why wouldn't he accept me, was his opening premise. If I gave him a reason to be distant, he'd make his distance at that point. But no need to do that prematurely. On the second day, he found the need to speak up.

"Mr. Rogue, you need to listen."

"What, Jason?" I asked.

"You need to listen. You are saying to much; instead you need to listen."

I paused to consider this. This kid I thought was disengaged was telling me how I should behave. Really? I almost responded from a defensive position. But, then something rich came over me as I took a breath and I stepped back. I listened.

For 20 minutes I didn't say anything. I listened to the kids talking to each other. I watched Jason and saw the progress coming in his rug. I did my best to disappear into the background and let the room find its own rhythm. I heard 3 kids ask Jason questions. He responded with actions and showed them what to do. The elder came by at one point and spoke in Navajo in clear, simple terms to Jason and a young girl named Leena.

Jason turned his attention to the elder without looking in her eyes. He was watching her hands as she spoke. I saw that his detachment was respect. That his demeanor was one of rapt attention and focused intellect. This kid knew his stuff. He'd learned more than any kid in the room and was acting as a teaching assistant. The elder had already brought him in for support, without a formal process, or a test, or an announcement. He just took on the role and excelled.

That day I found Jason at lunch and sat with him. We didn't say a lot. I was listening. We shared a meal together. That was a good start.

At the end of the first day, I met Alice. Rather, Alice introduced herself to me. As soon as the programming lessons were over and we had dismissed the kids for the day, she walked right over to me.

"Mr. Rogue, I'm Alice. Hello!" She smiled and held out her hand.

"Hello, Alice. Nice to meet you." I replied, with a smile right back at her.

"I want to thank you. My whole family wants to thank you." As she spoke, little Leena from the rug weaving class walked up beside Alice. "What you are teaching is very valuable. We have never had an opportunity like this. Thank you for bringing this work to our school."

"On behalf of everyone in the Bridges Program, you are very welcome. It's not just me. I'm just one teacher."

"I am confident my sister and I, and all the kids, will learn a lot from the elders and from you computer teachers. This is a life changing experience."

"You are confident about a lot of things." I said with a smile.

Alice smiled back. "Thank you. We'll see you tomorrow."

A teenage boy listened to this exchange from near the doorway. He walked out with Alice. I couldn't remember his name from class, but the next day, I watched him. He was Earl, in the basket group. After that first day, he opened up during lab time. He would call

Steve or I over with questions. He wasn't having trouble following. He had questions that extended what we had done, anticipated the next step of the lesson or what we would be doing the next day. He asked questions about things not in our curriculum. Clearly he was hungry for an advanced course in coding.

"Earl, can I talk to you?" I asked near the end of lunch. There was a gap between lunch and lab time to allow the students some unstructured time to socialize.

Earl excused himself from a conversation with Alice. "Yes, Mr. Rogue." As we stepped aside to talk, he spoke up. "I'm sorry I am asking so many questions. I will stop bothering you and the teachers."

"Earl, please don't stop," I looked him in the eye with a soft expression. "You are doing nothing wrong. In fact, Bill and I want to make you an offer. After lunch each day, please come to the lab early. You clearly get the coding ideas each day and want to learn more. So, we'll teach you. We have some other tools, more powerful languages you can learn. We want to help you move along in your coding."

Earl didn't respond right away. He was thinking, taking the offer seriously. He looked up at me, some tension on his face. He was smiling a bit, but some reluctance held him back. "Uh....Mr. Rogue..." He trailed off.

"Earl, no need to give me an answer now. Think about it. Talk to Alice. Just come some day, any day, after lunch. We will be there."

"Ok. Thank you." Earl let a smile build in his face. He was going to say something more. But, he just smiled, nodded his head, and went back to the group from lunch.

Earl didn't show up the next day. But, he did show up eventually, with Alice. He came in while she lingered at the doorway.

Bill said, "Earl, hello! Alice, come in please and sit down at a machine. Great to see you both! I assume you both want to learn some more coding?!" Bill smiled warmly at Alice, then Earl.

These two were a package, we weren't sure why or how, but clearly they were a package. That was fine. We knew by then that Alice was strong in math and a hard worker. This was not meant to be an exclusive offer. It was great to have any of the kids eager for extending their learning.

Chapter Five

TAKING A WALK

"You want to go for a walk?" Steve asked after dinner one night. There was plenty of sunlight left, and not much to do when we weren't teaching. So, a walk sounded great.

Steve was not in on the Navajo Project, not working for the Agency. Clearly, Bill and Hal had not brought him into the fold. If Bill had tried to do so at Caltech and failed, then Steve wouldn't be here at all - too risky. So, they had chosen not to bring him in yet. Maybe after Bridges they would make the move.

Either way I couldn't talk to him about the young recruits. Damn, I really wanted to talk to him about the recruits.

He led me behind the housing quad toward a butte back behind the parking lot, maybe 200 yards from the school.

We had to get past a fence. There were modestly maintained fences here and there in this desert landscape.

"Is this someone's property," I asked, as we found a gap in the fence we could exploit.

Houses were far apart from each other out here, so it was hard to tell who maintained the fences and why.

"Someone's property?" Steve responded. "That's a tricky question. You see, the Navajo look at property differently than you or I. They don't feel like they own property. Instead, the property owns them. If they were brought into this world as part of a family living in an area, then they are there to protect that area."

"Wow. Such a simple flip, but so powerful as well. I suppose that explains why so many stay and live on the reservation, despite the difficulty with finding work and making a living. Someone who moves to a nearby town is in some ways abandoning their job to protect the property that raised them."

"Yeah. That is one dynamic, certainly. There are others at play with people staying on the reservation too. The youngest generation is losing some of those deeper ties to the land and culture, so more and more are leaving the land."

Steve went on for a minute. He was so quiet that when he had some momentum for a story, I usually let him go. I figured something important was driving the story.

"Their view of property helps explain why houses are so far apart too. The Diné, as they call themselves, feel a responsibility for protecting all the land they have domain over. So, when the large reservation was established with only a few thousand Navajo, they needed to spread out to protect the land. To share the duty. So, while this area looks remote and isolated, you will hardly ever go too far without finding a home here or there. Instead of clustering into towns and having wide open land around the town, they simply have distributed themselves across the land with lots of space in between families."

"And what do people do for a living?"

"One of the biggest things that people do is raising sheep. Which is another reason for the distances. You can't have too many herds of sheep close to each other in this desert landscape. There would be nothing to graze on. But, people have found a wide range of jobs from being teachers, to running businesses. Employment is fairly diverse out here."

We kept walking toward the rock formation behind the school. The land was sloping upward, bringing us higher to meet the base of the rock formation.

"Is this a butte or a mesa?" I asked.

"How would I know?" Steve responded. I looked at him. He smiled and said, "Yeah, of course I know. So, a butte is smaller than a mesa. What exact size difference tips you from a butte to a mesa is up for debate. Some folks say that if there is water on top, or you could graze cattle on it, then it is a mesa, otherwise it is a butte. So, all the famous formations out here, like the mittens, are buttes."

"So, I would guess that this formation we are walking up here is a mesa," I said. "It stretches pretty far off that way, and it seems to have some depth to it. This feels pretty big, like enough vegetation is up here for grazing some animals."

Steve paused and thought. "Yeah, I'd call this a mesa, too. Mesa's are younger formations, having been cut more recently in geologic time. Buttes are basically what's left of an old mesa. Let's call this a mesa then."

It wasn't a hard climb, there were relatively well-warn paths. While some of the sides of the mesa had dramatic drop-offs, it was also a large enough feature that you could find cutouts here and there where some natural process had worn away a pathway of sorts. Maybe animals and people coming up and down had done some of that wear and tear.

We got to the top by actually walking into the mesa. Looking from a distance, it doesn't look like a mesa would have an inside. But, these pathways that open up when you get close often lead you to an interior area, midway up from the desert floor, but still with rock around you. You could see how pools of water, or small ponds might form back in there allowing for some vegetation to grow and the ability to graze animals.

"So, this is the land these kids grow up on. Such a unique place. I can see some of how it impacts who they are."

"You seem really interested in the kids and their lives," said Steve.

It was my time to tell a story, but I had to remember not to share with Steve my real intent.

"Yeah. You know the concept of teaching the programming and math is what drew me here. But, as I learned more about life here, and once I landed in this beautiful, but barren location, I became fascinated by these people. These kids have such a unique background - all the aspects of modern life around them, but living in this island of tradition. People are not living like throwbacks lost to time. These are modern lifestyles. But, centered on some traditional values, like the property ownership idea you described. I mean, man, that just gives someone a really unique perspective."

Steve was sizing me up this whole time, not just listening, but evaluating what was coming out of my mouth. Steve's a smart guy. He's likely to pick up on some of what the Navajo Project is this summer. I have to believe Hal is going to take the opportunity to invite him into the Agency after this.

I went on. "These kids are just fascinating to observe and to get to know. How they interact with each other. How they treat and interact with their elders - a rich dose of respect, but also a playful spirit. How they interact with you and me, and Bill. And like any group of young kids, they all have such a range of personalities. I just want to understand their world view. Try to take something home with me from this experience."

We had made our way up to the top of the mesa by this point, and had kind of doubled-back so we were looking back at the school to our East, and the tribal park off further behind it.

"Wow. What a view! You've been up here before? No wonder you wanted to go for a walk. Man, this is beautiful. I feel like I can see for 10 miles in each direction."

"It's actually closer to 20. There's just so little in the way, views go on for miles."

I could see the two isolated roads that came together at the high school. Highway 163, the highway we had come in on went basically North to South. To the North was Mexican Hat. I could see much of the path we had taken to get from there that first day, past a number of buttes. To the South was Arizona. I didn't know exactly where the border was, but our view was vast enough, I knew the border was in view. The highway just headed off that direction and disappeared over a small hill.

Another road led East to West. Behind us it led to the small trading post and campground. Then it was a dead end into a mesa. To the East, it led to the tribal park, with a parking lot and information center. I could see that entire road from our modest height above the valley.

The school was in the Southwest corner of the intersection, taking up a tidy plot of land between the building itself and the athletic fields. If this were a suburban school, the other three corners would have strip malls, big box stores and lots of traffic. But, instead, it was just wide open land leading in these three other directions. It made the existence of the school at this spot seem that much more special, sort of surreal. A community had clearly placed an uneven emphasis on educating their youth, on making an opportunity for these kids that would not be there otherwise. It taught them the skills to work and survive outside the reservation, leading some to actually leave. But it also said to them, you can get everything you need here - we are investing in you as a part of this community. Which message were the kids receiving more strongly?

Hopefully Bridges was strengthening that second message. Yet, I was here specifically to lay a path for a handful to leave. Man, I was conflicted.

Across from us, beyond the school, but not all the way to the tribal park, there was a large mesa rising up, almost parallel to the one we had climbed on this side. Between these two larger formations, it gave the sense of a valley of sorts. The road leading South to Arizona basically traced a line down the middle of that natural valley.

I felt small. I was in a land of giants. The view from up top seemed like a sandbox for giants. The buttes were rocks that a giant had found and laid out in formation. They were not structured on a human scale, but on a scale 100 times larger. It was humbling and inspiring all at once.

As we were up there, it got late enough that the sun started going down.

"This is why I suggested we walk up here," said Steve, as the orange hues of the sunset started forming.

The red hue of the sand and rocks came to life. It was like the rocks were on fire. Or like they were lit up from the inside. The sunset lighting fulfilled the promise of the lifeless stones, creating an unforgettable vista. Once again, I felt transported to an alien land.

I started to open up to Steve a bit more about how the kids in this program were special.

"This land, these vistas, the colors, the lighting, the scale, the intense beauty. This is what the kids on the reservation grow up with. It is their everyday normal. Their memories are littered with beautiful scenes at sunset or sunrise, storms rolling across the horizon like a curtain being drawn, buttes bursting from the earth like fingers reaching to the sky. Their imaginations and palettes of visual metaphors include a rich set of snapshots of intensity. I can feel it in talking to them and working with them. You know what I mean?"

Steve was quiet, contemplative. It felt like he paused for ever. Then, he turned to me with a big smile, he thumped me on the shoulder with a laugh, then headed back down.

The walk that evening left a big impression on me.

That Friday, Hal came back to the school. He taught up in Salt Lake City during the week, but had set aside his weekends to support the Bridges Program and help us keep it moving forward.

When Hal arrived at noon, he said hello, but quickly reported to Dr. Squire's office to have lunch and catch up. He wanted to hear from her how the program was going.

After lunch, he checked in with the elders, hearing stories from the week, getting reports about how the kids were doing. For our last half hour of computer lab work, he came in to see how we were doing. He walked around to coach the kids on their programming and their visual designs. When it was time to wrap up, many of the kids came over to Hal with questions and stories from the week. While Bill and Steve and I were closing down the lab, we heard him asking the kids how we were doing. We couldn't hear the responses, but we knew we'd hear from Hal later.

He gathered us up in his car and drove us up toward Mexican Hat. We were going to have a real meal on Hal. I don't think this was covered in the grant, he just wanted to take care of his instructors.

"Anthony and Steve, this place we're going to eat is awesome." Bill told us. "The ingredients they get, the flavors, the menu. This place would compete well in any mid-sized city like Salt Lake. It is amazing food, bar none."

Steve looked dubious. "C'mon, Steve, I'm a vegetarian too," I said. "I'm sure they'll have something tasty. Don't you trust Bill?"

He had every reason not to trust Bill. Bill was always playing jokes. This was right up his alley. For all we knew we were headed to a greasy spoon best experienced late at night while drunk.

"Here it is!" Hal pulled up to the house-turned-restaurant. The sign out front read "The Inn."

The decor and menu were reassuring. Bill was being straight. I ordered veggie chili and Steve had their tasty veggie burger. The food was presented in a clean, yet homey manner. It was filling, yet felt healthy, fresh and light. This was the best meal I'd had since coming to Utah.

Hal wanted to talk business at dinner. He didn't spend any time discussing the feedback he got about our work. He had confidence in us and we knew that.

"Tell me about the kids. Who stands out, who are the hard workers? Who has an interesting story?"

Bill told Hal about Earl, his voracious appetite for programming, and the progress he was making. I followed up by telling about Jason and how he helped me learn how to get out of the way.

"Alice has real talent. With the programming, math and crafts, yes. But also with the other kids - I can see a leader there." Steve jumped in as if he knew where we were headed with Project Navajo.

"Yes, indeed." I said. "Alice was next on my list to tell you about, Hal. Steve, tell us what you saw with Alice."

"She is in my beadwork group. The very first day, she was introducing herself to Leena, the elder for the class. Since that moment, she has been a hub on which Leena has based her teaching. And Alice speaks up all the time to provide the view of the kids back to Leena. She is a natural bridge between the local elders and the kids."

"And her coding is right in step with Earl during our lunchtime lessons." I added. "She came along as a part of the package, but she shows us daily that she belongs there."

We spent the meal talking about those 3 and all the other kids. It was clear these three were on a different plateau from the rest of the kids.

After making our way back to the school housing, Steve went out for an evening hike. He headed straight up the road toward the tribal park.

"Pull up a chair, Anthony." Hal urged. "Ok, you all found the three kids we already had in mind. They are passing each hurdle with flying colors."

"Yes, they are. I assumed it would take so much longer to identify them."

"You've got to move on having a conversation with the parents. Bill can't do it, he's too close to me. If they trace this effort back through me, the whole program is in jeopardy."

I had my marching orders. Time for me to step up and get this moving.

Chapter Six

FAMILY PLAN

I was able to meet all three families that week, after lessons had ended for the day. The families did not show much surprise. They had a mix of pride and concern. Their kids were talented enough to build this program. Yet, the parents had memories of government officials who came to them when they were young, taking them away from family - not for special training based on their talents, but to wrench the culture and language of their people out of them.

This shameful history of Anglo treatment of Native Americans made my job that much harder. That learning program of years ago had started when they were young, with no real parental or tribal consent. It was more clear this new project was an opportunity for a few young people to find a new path to adulthood than it was a plan to change the tribe. I gave the parents some room to think about it. They could reach out to me, or I'd check back in with them in a few days.

The next day, I got a call. "Alice is excited about this opportunity. And we support her taking this leap."

"Oh, that is great news! Thanks for calling me."

"Thank you for awarding her the scholarship and special training. You have made a great choice - clearly you can see the great talent we've witnessed throughout her life. Let us know what to do next."

"Ok. The Monterey Institute will send you a packet of materials for entering the school. This is so exciting."

The other families never contacted me, so I called Earl's parents first.

"Mr. Begay, hello! This is Anthony Rogue. I am calling about the scholarship I talked to you about on Monday."

"Yes," was all I heard in reply.

"So, now that you have thought about it as a family, what do you think?"

"Yes, I said. Earl can go."

"Oh, that is great news! We are excited he will be joining the program."

"Thank you. Good-bye."

"Thank you!" The conversation was over, quick. It felt unsatisfying. There seemed to be a bit of reluctance there, but it may just have been an effort to be efficient and clear in their response. However it came about, the answer was a Yes.

When I called Jason's family, the conversation was quick, but not such a good outcome.

"Mr. Rogue, we have talked about this a lot during the last few days. Our answer for Jason is No. Jason's place is here."

"Mr. Dodge, I understand your concerns. Can I come over so we can talk more about this? What questions can I help answer?"

"We have the answers we need. Now you have our answer. We don't want to meet again about it. Thank you."

Well, that was a defeat. Earl and Alice had great talents and would do well. But, we need more than 2 kids to make this program work. And Jason was my secret weapon. I know there is something inside ready to blossom. He'll do well wherever he takes his life. I really wanted him to rocket forward and take our project beyond our expectations. I knew he could do it.

During a break on Friday, Jason came over to me.

"Anthony, I really want the scholarship. I will be a part of the program."

"Wait, what? Your father told me a clear no yesterday. What changed his mind?"

"Nothing changed his mind. I'm telling you I want to go."

"Jason, I am sure you do. But, this is a family decision. We won't offer the scholarship without your parents agreeing."

"I don't understand. I turn 18 in a month. I am an adult and I can make my choices. I want the scholarship."

"Jason, I am glad you have this passion for the program. This is not a legal issue of who has the right to decide for you. This is a rule within the program. We are not going to let a young man like yourself participate without family support. It's just the way it is. You have to talk them into changing their mind."

Jason was disappointed. He seemed confused and let down by my response. But, there was a fire there. So, I had new confidence this would work out.

That afternoon, Hal arrived for his second visit. I gave him the update on the recruits. He got on the phone immediately about Jason. He didn't call the Dodges. As he said before, he could not be lobbying for this personally. It would undermine the longer term Bridges program. He called Monterey to talk to Dr. van Gotsche.

"Van Gotsche is going to present the scholarships on our final day of Bridges. I've asked him to come a day early to talk to the Dodge family."

"That's great. Do you think he'll be able to do it?"

Hal smiled. "I know he will." And that was our last conversation about that.

Jason spent the week a bit distracted. We had lunch together a few times. He seemed mostly himself, but there was something he was holding back. I got the feeling he either had not tried to convince his folks, or had tried and failed. I wanted so much to help him then and there. To give him a lifeline. To call his parents. But, I was waiting for Prof. van Gotsche. Man, he needed to be good. We needed to help this kid. I had too much invested in Jason to walk away.

Van Gotsche flew in Wednesday night. He was going to award the scholarships on Friday. So, he had Thursday to work things out with the Dodges.

"Welcome to Bridges!" I said.

"Thanks! This place is in the middle of nowhere," replied van Gotsche.

"Yeah, well I think that was the point of the reservation system."

"Ah, right! Got it. This is exciting work you guys are doing. It reminds me of this project I consulted on..."

"So, what help do you need tomorrow?"

"I'm sorry? Help?"

"Do you want one of us to come with you to see the Dodges? Or maybe an elder from the school to guide you?"

"I'm not worried. So, I was consulting on this project when the local sheriff came to visit..."

"Well, I'm happy to come along?"

"Thanks." He gave a bit of a strained smile. "So, the sheriff comes in and I am totally at a loss..."

Bill was listening to his story intently and smiling. It was all gibberish to me. This guy was meant to save the day for Jason, to get him into the Project with our other two recruits. And he didn't even want the background story. Or any help the next day. I was so focused on what Jason needed, I couldn't understand why he wasn't there too.

But, then, I remembered what Jason had said that first week. "Mr. Rogue, you are saying too much and need to listen."

So, I stopped running through my concerns in my head. I stopped saying all of those doubting, panicked things to myself. I took a deep breath. And I listened.

"The sheriff really did that?" Bill asked.

"That was just the beginning. So, the next day, we get to work again, and there's the sheriff..."

Van Gotsche disappeared on Thursday. He had his plan and approach for working with the Dodges and didn't see a need for any local support.

Classes were frantic, as this was the last day to complete class projects. Rugs had to be complete. Designs on the computer needed to be complete. Baskets, beadwork. The elders had no concerns about what was done when. The kids would complete projects after the program if necessary. No need to rush. But Bill, Steve, and I wanted to have our ducks in a row. There was a community sharing on Friday. We were so proud of the work of all the kids. We wanted their parents to see the accomplishment.

I pulled aside Earl, Alice, and Jason at lunch, asking them to take on a special role for Friday. They were happy and proud to be asked, stepping up to be leaders. Jason had that chastened look on his face, worrying about not getting the scholarship. But, he didn't let that get in the way of working with the other two on the sharing celebration.

Later that night, I got a call from Jason's mom.

"Mr. Rogue. I want you to know that Jason is excited to take part in your project in Monterey. He is excited to be offered the scholarship and gladly accepts the scholarship and the opportunity."

"Mrs. Dodge. Thank you so much for the call. This is such great news. I just thought you and his dad had decided it would not be a good choice for him. What changed?"

"Jason has our blessing, Mr. Rogue." I could hear the smile on her face as she said the words. But, she never explained any further.

"Thank you. Thank you so much."

Friday, the sharing celebration kicked off. Alice, Earl, and Jason beamed with pride as they opened the celebration with a traditional welcome and prayer. They brought each of the younger students up to present their craft work and their computer design. The kids all had a chance to share their favorite moment of the program.

Then, Alice called up the tribal elders who had taught the traditional crafts.

"We thank you for your gifts to us. For your wisdom and patience. And for the math we learned from all of you."

Earl and Jason presented each of them with flowers as a thank you.

Then, Earl called up Bill, Steve, and me.

"We thank you for your gifts to us. For the technology and the inspiration. And for the math we learned from all of you."

Jason and Alice presented us each with beautiful beaded bracelets.

Steve called up Hal.

"We thank you for your gifts to us. For your vision and organization. And for the math we learned from you."

Bill and I presented Hal with a book of photos from the program and printouts of the student projects. It had Bridges written on the front.

Finally, Hal called up Prof. van Gotsche.

"We thank you for your gifts to us. For your questions and support. And for the learning we shared along the way."

I presented him with a photo of the school and the valley behind. Prof. van Gotsche was touched. He accepted the gift humbly.

"Let me say a few words on this important day. When I was a young man, I lived with the Quechua people of Peru. I learned many things from my time there. I studied their language, both to learn it myself and to use it as material for linguistic research. I learned what love was and met my wife there. I learned about this fine people and their history. But, the main thing I learned was that I am not Quechua. I am not of them. I never was and I never will be. As an impressionable young man, I thought I could become a part of them - to let my Dutch self fade away until I was accepted as one of them.

"I was reminded every week that I was not Quechua. No one needed to say anything, I could just feel it. And it really bothered me. Then, one day, out of the north came a flock of birds. They were on the move, spending a few months in one place, then picking up when the seasons changed.

"It reminded me that I was a transient. While I was comfortable among the Quechua - I would not stay that way forever. I would need to move on. I always had, and I would once again. So I said to myself, Lev, it is time to move on. I told Elsa my plan and asked her to marry me. Together we moved on.

"Some people are meant to leave their home, to move on, to experience other ways of living. It is in this spirit, that I come with the offer of a new path for three young people. I am awarding the van Gotsche scholarship to 3 participants in the Bridges Program. A bridge from your learning here in Monument Valley to learn more, experience more in Monterey, CA, at the Monterey Institute of International Studies. This scholarship goes to Alice Bluehouse, Earl Begay, and Jason Dodge. Congratulations!"

The crowd erupted in excitement for these three young people. Clearly, the community loved them and was proud of this accomplishment and opportunity. The joy at witnessing the sharing ceremony exploded into excitement about the scholarships. This was a proud day for the community of Monument Valley High School.

Chapter Seven

AILEEN

When I woke up that morning, I didn't know my whole life was about to change. I didn't know this would be the day I met Aileen. How could I know? I wish I had known - I could have been ready for this life changing earthquake.

Coming from Utah, I stayed with Adam and Lexie in Santa Cruz, unloading my U-Haul in their garage, crashing on their couch. Adam was another Techer, my best friend from Caltech. He had also been recruited from Tech by the Agency. And now we'd be living 45 minutes apart in Central California, while he worked on his PhD and I worked on the Navajo Project. Adam's place was essentially a safe house for me, to get my bearings and get ready for Monterey. While I was starting a Masters in language teaching at MIIS and working on the Navajo Project, Adam had his own assignment while embedded at UCSC. Either way, we'd be hanging out, living so close. Meeting Lexie that weekend had been fun. I could see how she and Adam made a good partnership. She and I were already finding common ground. It helped that she was a Jersey Girl and a fan of Bruce Springsteen.

But, with the weekend behind me, it was time to make my way to Monterey and find housing. So, that morning, I drove Adam's car to Monterey and hit campus. The town was pretty. The drive down had been along the Monterey Bay, waves and ocean breezes on my right as I drove, fields of garlic, strawberries and numerous other crops on my left. The air was moist, cool, and sweet. I could get used to this place.

Campus consisted of a dozen or so Spanish style buildings just 2 blocks up the hill from downtown Monterey. Monterey was dense but small. There were few tall buildings, but the hills and streets were packed with houses, businesses, and apartment buildings. So, the campus provided a bit of modest open space between its buildings. There were courtyards and meeting areas. It was an academic island tucked into a tourist destination town.

Parking on campus, I headed toward the housing office. I had heard I was walking into a great environment for a single, young man. Language teaching was a field of mostly women. Starting a program for language teachers meant I would be mostly surrounded by women in my classes. The inverse of the Caltech experience. I was admittedly excited. But, how could I know literally the first person I met would be the one.

I walked into the Housing Office looking for apartment help. I expected to find a full time campus staff member who would help all the students find a place to live. As I said hello, she looked up and said, "Hi! I'm Aileen. Nice to meet you!"

She had shoulder length brown-red hair. Her face lit up as she said hello. Her hazel eyes had a generous feeling, a natural helper looking to connect me with housing. Her smile was beautiful, and she used it often in our 3 minute chat.

"Hi..." There was a noticeable pause. It felt like an eternity to me. Was I that obvious? Could I really not put more than two words together.

"Are you looking for housing?" She asked.

"Yes," I said, nodding. Then nothing.

"Do you know the area?" Aileen continued.

"Nope." This time, I mustered a dumb grin at least.

She smiled. "Ok, sit down and let's get started."

I sat down mutely. I smiled and an internal dialogue kicked off.

Good, I 'm going to get to spend some time with her. Maybe this could be our first date?

First date, she doesn't know who you are. You've barely said a word. At this point, she probably assumes you are an international student with limited English. C'mon, snap out of it!

Aileen pulled out a map of Monterey and showed me the different towns and neighborhoods - near campus, New Monterey by Cannery Row, Pacific Grove, Seaside.

"I need to stay near campus, because I don't have a car." I finally strung something meaningful together.

"Then your best bets are New Monterey, Pacific Grove, and the hills just above campus. Some people bike in from Seaside, or Carmel, but you want to be near enough you can do study groups and other meetings with classmates."

"Got it, great. Now, where do I find a paper to track down some listings?"

"Oh, actually, we have a great board out front where people post notes about places they are renting," Aileen said as she stood up. "Come on, I'll show ya!"

She got up and led me out into the courtyard. I watched her fit and active body as she led me the twenty feet to the housing board. She wore longish shorts, a simple T-shirt, and a fleece to stay warm. She was not showing off her body. Her skin was clear and healthy looking, not tanned and leathery, but a nice, creamy white Northern European skin tone with some natural hints of red cheeks. All and all, she really did glow like she took care of herself, but didn't mess with pounds of make-up to hide the natural beauty underneath.

I'm sure I was smiling as we walked out to the board of apartment postings. I listened intently, hung on every word she said. By this point, I was somewhat myself, had snapped out of it and was telling little jokes here and there. Her light laughter and smile at my lame attempts at humor pulled me in closer to her charms.

Aileen pointed out a few postings that looked good, and commented on their rent prices, giving me a sense of what was affordable or an expected rent.

"Do you have what you need now?" she asked, with a genuine sense of concern. There was no rush in her voice, but I could tell she felt like it was time to wrap up.

"I guess so... Thanks so much!" I said somewhat lamely. I was trying my best to come up with a reason to keep talking to her, to keep her here, busy with me. Nothing came, so I let her walk away. I watched as she walked away. As she was about to turn the corner, she looked back and saw me watching her. I felt a bit caught and smiled with a bit of embarrassment. She gave a similar shy smile in return. Was there something there? Had she seen something she liked in me already? After that bumbling start, could I have actually made a good impression? Nah, probably not. But, maybe?

I looked over the board and found 5 possible places to call about. As I was wrapping up, she came out again.

"Oh, I forgot. You are looking at the best time. Most students arrive in August and half the places are taken. So, be patient if you can - you'll find a great place. Don't grab the first thing you look at."

"Wow. Ok, thanks." I smiled and our eyes met. She smiled back. There was a pause, both of us lingering. Was I seeing something in those eyes? She blinked her eyes shut, turned, and made her way back into the housing office with a quick step.

I was distracted for a moment, watching where she had been, the path she had walked back to the office. I could still see her in my mind's eye. She was kind of a cross between Kate Winslet and Annette Bening. A Scandinavian face with a bright smile like Annette Bening on top of Kate Winslet's frame.

I sat down to eat a carrot from my backpack and collect my thoughts. Then, I made a few calls.

I came back to town the next few days, continuing to look. Making calls, checking out rooms and apartments. Half were filled, others were too far. Some were really small when I looked at them, not worth the money being asked for.

Each time I came looking, I would pop into the Housing Office, planning to say hi to Aileen. She was never around. There was another student there helping. While she was nice and supportive, she was not Aileen. I began to wonder if I'd imagined her. I learned later that she had gone back home for a few weeks for a friend's wedding.

I found a place in New Monterey. It was a 10 minute bike ride or 30 minute walk from campus - very reasonable. Good rent. Sharing one room with a guy who worked as a nurse in town. We had little in common but got along fine as roommates. His patterns and habits never got in my way. And mine never got in his way.

But, still no sign of Aileen.

Chapter Eight

STANFORD PICNIC

Was I doing the right thing?

How could I know we were heading for an "oh sh$t" moment? Really, you never know when you are headed for one. You just live your life, and they happen when they happen.

There I was, hopping on the back of the motorcycle of my friend Doug Krieg. I had known Doug for years. But, in some ways, no one really knew Doug. He held things back. Like the year we were roommates and he kept me from discovering that he had gotten his nipple pierced. Of my friends from Caltech, I probably knew the least about Doug - felt some distance and thus less of a close bond with him. Yet, he was still in that circle of 6 of us - and I was going to continue to discover over the years how good a friend he really is.

I had never seen Doug ride his motorbike. I'd never been on even a short jaunt around the block with him. But, here I was, hopping on the back, ready to ride 60 miles north along California highways. Not just any simple highway, mind you, but Highway 17 over the hill from Santa Cruz to San Jose. I strapped the helmet on and thought, "Am I crazy?"

The internal dialogue continued. "No. I know Doug. He does not do anything halfway. He studies, prepares, focuses, and becomes an expert at whatever he is doing. The man is a machine. He is not taking this trip lightly. I can trust him."

So, off we went, on our way to a picnic with other Caltech grads near Stanford. I had not seen these friends in years and was looking forward to this. If I had had a car in Monterey, I'm sure we would have been in that on our way. So, Doug's bike it was. At a stop, he leaned back and told me to be sure I relaxed and left the steering to him - don't use my weight to move the bike, or it would throw him off. Ok, he was taking this seriously. So, I would too.

Highway 17 leads from the ocean town of Santa Cruz up into the Santa Cruz Mountains. It winds it's way to an elevation of 1,808 ft, then drops you back down into the heart of Silicon Valley, all in the span of 21 miles. The wealth and opportunity of Silicon Valley rivals Wall Street and Hollywood. But, the Valley focuses on technology and engineering, not finances or entertainment. People build things here. And more often than not money grows on trees in this valley - no longer a valley of orchards for agriculture and fruit production. Now, these are orchards of innovation, growth and wealth, spread among hundreds of thousands of brilliant engineers from around the world.

Santa Cruz embodies the beauty of California's natural wealth. Ocean views, hillside forests home to migrating monarchs, ancient redwoods, and thousands of young college students. Surfers dot the waves off the shore, at this northern tip of the dramatic Monterey Bay. An old time boardwalk amusement park lights up downtown with laughter and music. Fine food, wine, creative artists and a walkable community attract a wide range of people. This community draws the attention of the wealth sitting just over the hill.

Many people dream of the Santa Cruz lifestyle fueled by the wealth available in Silicon Valley. And Highway 17 connects the two dots. Traffic each day stretches the capacity of this mountain byway. It's been widened and improved over the years, but in the end, it was never meant to carry so many vehicles back and forth so quickly. The first time I ever experienced it, I was driving a U-Haul truck solo about 30% full of my modest belongings. I am not a truck driver. I had brought the U-Haul from Denver, through Nevada along the loneliest highway in America, over the Sierra's into central California, to be topped off with Highway 17. I think that last stretch of Highway 17 was what scared me the most about that drive.

So, here we were, making our way on this highway with two guys on top of a solid, but modest bike. This was no Gull Wing built for two to travel cross country. Doug had on his leathers. He had encouraged me to wear jeans and closed toe shoes, a modest second skin to protect my own skin in the event of a wipeout. I thought that was a little silly, but I complied. I knew Doug wouldn't let it go - he was very particular about process and procedure - doing things a certain way. If he had done the research and learned of a specific, desirable approach - if he had analyzed that and incorporated it into his own approach to that activity, riding a motorcycle or designing microprocessor chips - then that was the way he wanted to do it. So, I showed up in jeans and hiking boots - both protective and not too unusual to wear to a picnic.

We made our way up into the Santa Cruz mountains. First the foothills East of the town, but quickly climbing into genuine mountainous terrain. This was a paved, well-maintained highway - so don't think dirt road, but mountainous. And while the road certainly had some bends and windiness, it still climbed pretty directly up the mountains to the summit. I was having a good time on the bike. When I'd last rode one a few years earlier, it was just me driving a medium sized street bike. I had only just learned how to drive it with my roommate that summer in San Diego. It was his bike. My folks had always said that we could not buy a motorbike while under their roof. And once at college, if we bought one, we could say goodbye to their financial support during college. So, I had always dutifully stayed away from them. But, during this summer interning, I was going to a pickup basketball game with my roommate. When we stepped out to make our way there, he pulled out his motorcycle and said, "Hop on." I hesitated, but then pulled the helmet on and hopped on back. It was only literally a mile or two to the Y for the basketball game. While I was nervous to be on the back of the bike, I also enjoyed it. So, later that summer he showed me the basics of how to ride. I took the bike out in the neighborhood 2-3 times with his help and teaching.

Then, one day, that roommate was out of town for the weekend, and I had nothing going on, on Saturday. So, I borrowed the bike, hopped on, and rode up the California coast along Highway 1.

The PCH - Pacific Coast Highway - a legendary road. That was a fun afternoon - just me against the wind. Sure, I felt vulnerable, but I also felt more in touch with the road. I was more exposed to the elements - could feel the moist, sea air as I rode up and down the highway. I could smell the salt, the fish, the aroma of the sea as I made my way out of town and into beachfront stretches with fewer and fewer cars. I also tested the responsiveness of the bike a few times. You feel more in touch with the road because you can respond so quickly on a motorcycle. There is a merging of yourself, the bike and the road that you don't feel in a Dodge Charger or Toyota Tercel.

I only rode for an hour or two, still nervous about the "bad thing" happening, something going wrong. As I made my way back to the house where I rented a room, the last 3 miles of Highway 1 actually merged with Interstate 5. I had to merge onto the expressway and get up to 55 miles an hour. I had not been above 40 during the PCH exploration. There was no turning back, so I accelerated up to highway speeds, but hugged that slow lane. Constantly checking all around me, nerves going crazy. It seemed like everyone else on the highway was going 80 miles an hour.

Then someone came buzzing next to me in the second lane going 20 mph faster than anyone else around. I swear he was hitting 100 or more. Where were the cops? John and Ponch needed to be here, catching all these speed demons? Finally, I saw my exit ahead. That stretch of the last half mile after the green sign appeared signaling the exit up ahead took what felt like 20 minutes. But, I made it there, gently pulled off the road and hit the surface streets again. Whew!

So, back on Highway 17 with Doug, it was such a different experience. He was both more competent and more confident on his bike. He knew what he was doing, he knew his bike, he knew the road. All things I was missing years before in San Diego. Because of that, he was taking the road at regular speeds. When cars in front of us were hesitating or slowing down, he quickly changed lanes, taking advantage of a motorcycle's more agile handling. I was experiencing a faster, more adrenaline-filled motorcycle experience than I ever had on my own. Yet, I needed to trust Doug to drive, to let go of some control myself. I did. I was able to relax, look around, and just enjoy the experience of the wind on my body and that close feeling to the road.

The mountainous scenery along Highway 17 is nice. Driving into Santa Cruz a few months earlier, I had not been able to focus on the scenery. I had a U-Haul truck, making these curves and taking steep declines into the coastal town. It was a white-knuckler just to get across the hill from Los Gatos. There was no way I'd let myself get distracted by scenery. This time I could leave the driving to someone else and enjoy the views.

We quickly made our way past the coastal Redwoods and up to Scotts Valley. There were a surprising number of people turning off for Scotts Valley. It felt like we were in the middle of nowhere, on the side of a mountain. But, people lived and worked in this area - there must be something of a small town hiding off the highway here. It was a Saturday, so traffic was relatively light. That meant there were certainly cars on the road - Highway 17 was never dead, except perhaps truly in the middle of the night. Yet, there was no stop and go like rush hour on a weekday. Traffic was flowing, as fast as the curves and climbing would allow. There were just a lot of cars flowing fast. And having the power and agility of a motorcycle, we were pushing the limits, going faster than most people around us. Doug would make his way back and forth between the lanes to keep us moving ahead, passing any number of other cars. It did not feel like we were driving with wild abandon. Just keeping a steady pace, not letting others determine our speed.

After Scotts Valley, things got a bit more curvy, like switchbacks for a stretch. We were clearly making the climb now, making our way up as quickly as the terrain would allow. We got to the peak of the mountain pass. I could see the green highway signs for Summit Rd. coming up, a sure sign we had reached the high point of Highway 17. But, as we got closer to Summit Rd., the traffic finally did begin to drag. We couldn't make our way between cars as easily. So, we ended up in the fast lane, in a bit of a line behind two other cars. The first car was a classic, red convertible. Perhaps it was a 1957 Thunderbird. That was the car my mom was in love with, and always wanted. Whatever it was, it was in good shape, running smoothly and looking good. Let's just say it was a Thunderbird for the sake of a colorful story. The driver had the top down and was clearly enjoying the day. We could see this car over the top of the sedan in front of us. The sedan was a brown foreign model, likely a Japanese car. Not terribly sexy, but solid and dependable. It had a bit of age on it, but was much newer than the convertible, and showed its age well.

We came to a bit of a straightaway, as the summit appeared. Then we were on a modest downhill stretch, allowing us a clear shot of both cars - the sedan and the Thunderbird. Suddenly, I heard a noise. I tensed up and looked ahead. The brown sedan was chugging along, but I could see a bit of smoke coming from the Thunderbird. The driver seemed to be slowing down a bit, so Doug instinctively did the same thing. Then, all-of-a-sudden, the hood of the convertible popped up. It went straight in the air, blocking the entire windshield of the Thunderbird. The driver did the only thing he could do and slammed the brakes. I could hear the squealing and smell the rubber. A split second later, a new noise as the brown sedan hit his brakes. He was so close to the Thunderbird, would he be able to stop quickly enough?

I barely had a chance to find out. I felt Doug tap our brakes to come closer to the speed of the cars in front of us. Suddenly, I felt us lurch to the right. Oh My! I remembered what Doug had told me early on. Don't use my body to steer the motorcycle. If I tried to turn one way or the other, I'd throw off Doug's driving. I'd either drag us back away from where he wanted us to go, or would overcompensate and send us in the right direction but at too steep of a turn. I felt myself grab on to him a bit tighter with my hands, but let the rest of my body go a bit, so it would just flow with the bike.

There was no room on our right for us to go all the way over to the next lane, but we couldn't stay where we were either. The Thunderbird was rapidly coming to a stop, the brown sedan had made bumper-to-bumper contact, and the car behind us was coming too fast to stop as well. There was soon to be a pileup of at least 3 cars, with us sandwiched in the middle.

But Doug pulled us expertly into the middle of the lanes. We didn't slam into the traffic still going at regular speeds to our right and we avoided ramming into the sedan in front of us. I heard crunching sounds as Doug pulled back on the throttle and got us back up to speed quickly. We shot past the sedan and Thunderbird without ever fully changing lanes.

I heard more crunching of fenders and screeching of brakes, with some swerving added to the mix. The lanes were starting to get tangled. Once he knew we were beyond the sedan and Thunderbird, Doug brought us back into our lane. He knew it was clear, because the pileup was effectively blocking the flow on it. By this point, my heart was in my throat. My grip was still tight on Doug, and I wasn't ready to loosen up. I was waiting for the other shoe to drop. Surely we were meant to hit something, drop to the pavement, get thrown off the bike. All those things you hear happen to people on motorcycles in a crash. My parents were right and I was going to be seriously hurt. I was just waiting for it to happen.

But nothing did happen. We settled back into highway speeds, perhaps 5 mph slower than before the crash. We kept moving, winding our way down the hills toward Los Gatos and San Jose. We were just riding to our picnic, as we had been a minute before. But, how? It was crazy. In the slow motion of the event, I had registered all the steps Doug took to make it through. Tapping the brakes, moving in the middle of the lanes (I was always annoyed when motorcycles used that middle non-lane to move ahead of me in traffic), putting on a burst of speed, then swerving back where the road was clear again. He had threaded the needle, literally. And he'd done it with barely a thought or hesitation, as if he'd practiced it.

It turned out Doug had practiced it. After a few more minutes, he called back to me. "You alright?"

"Yeah, I guess so." I answered tentatively. It was still hard to believe. My adrenaline rush was calming down, but I was still on high alert for something to happen. That bad thing that I was waiting for before. I couldn't let it go. "How'd we do that?" I said.

"Practice." Was Doug's answer.

I didn't get it. But, 10 minutes later, after we'd left Highway 17 and made our way to the 101 North through Santa Clara and Sunnyvale, Doug pulled over into a parking lot. We both stepped off the bike and took off our helmets. I was shaking a bit.

Doug told me that he practiced that. All the time. Actually, often on 101. He'd find times when the road was relatively clear, then he'd give himself an 'Oh shit' warning out of the blue. At that point, he'd tap the brakes, shift to the middle of the lanes, and speed ahead. He'd read about how to use the agility of a bike in an emergency situation. Then, he'd practiced, dozens, maybe hundreds of times. He'd never needed it before. But, today, it was exactly what we needed. And he was able to do it on instinct. I gave him a high five and said, "Thanks, man!"

"Do you need a bathroom break or a drink?" he asked.

"No man. What about you?"

"I'm good. Let's get to Stanford."

And off we went, riding the 20 minutes or so up the 101 to Stanford. We pulled into the parking lot, got off the bike and found our friends from Tech. Man, did we have a story to tell them. And a story to share over and over again.

Chapter Nine

AFTER THE PICNIC

He quickly looked around to make sure no one had spotted him. Then he stood up and brushed off the dirt. His tan shirt and pants allowed him to blend into the central California hills. Without thinking, his hands began disassembling the rifle. He dropped the cartridge out and unscrewed the silencer. Then the stock and barrel. Everything fit nicely into the lightweight case on the ground.

While his hands automatically dealt with the disassembly, his mind was racing. The Oligarchs would not be happy. This was twice the attempts had failed. The Oligarchs had little patience for failure. Fortunately, both attempts were expertly crafted to disguise the attempt itself. Because Rogue survived and wasn't even in the accident, the Agency would never look into this car crash. The local police wouldn't even think to investigate the Thunderbird's hood, never find the damage done by his two shots into the engine block. It would just be written off as a 50 year old car giving out.

He hadn't counted on the friend being such an expert bike rider. He'd have to find out more about this Doug Krieg. There were stories that Rogue had been brought into the Agency by the parents of a classmate. Perhaps this computer chip designer was the Caltech buddy with spooks for parents? But this bike rider couldn't be an Agent. The Oligarchs had cleared his background. No one at this Stanford picnic was an Agent. Just Rogue. That's why it was such a perfect chance to take him out. He left himself vulnerable. Believing in his cover so much he was over confident. Rogue was supposed to be one of the best in the Agency, but he was getting soft on this assignment.

The rifleman had thought that with no Agents around today, no one could disrupt this perfect plan. Yet, Rogue's buddy, Doug Krieg, saved the day. Why did the Oligarchs insist this appear accidental? He had plenty of ideas for staging accidents. But, straight assassination had always worked for these clients. Not this time. Why? ... His thoughts trailed off.

His phone was ringing as he got back to his own bike. They were expecting a report. Had they already learned some other way? Did someone spot Rogue further along Highway 17? Man, accountability was supreme with these guys.

"Schelletz. Go ahead."

A nervous pause.

"Right. The bike escaped. Yes, Rogue escaped. Krieg proved an expert driver. He could ride in Greymouth next month. The kid has skills. We had no idea."

Another pause.

"Of course. 0 for 2. No, not my typical standard."

"I ... I understand. I am grateful. I always want to satisfy the Oligarchs. One more chance to do that is certainly all I need. I'll be in touch soon with the plan. Thank you."

Chapter Ten

THE LAB

I started working with Dr. van Gotsche later in July.

"Call me Lev," he said once I settled into town.

"Got it. Anthony works for me - no need for a cover identity."

"Oh, I assumed Anthony Rogue was the cover. You mean it' s your real name?"

I just smiled.

The lab was such a great place to work. I was getting in at the ground floor of something, helping him build out his vision. A space for using technology to study language. But, a place that fostered interaction and connection, not isolation. He had theorized about ways to use technology to enhance and draw out interaction between students. Now he was going to build it and make it work. What a great environment for me to learn.

But, the real work was about getting ready for the kids from Monument Valley. They would be coming to town in 3 weeks for orientation. So, when the lab was empty, or over coffee in the evening, we would talk through the plan for their training. It started at the Monterey Institute - aka MIIS. This was good, because that would be their cover.

The kids would explore three things there. They would learn about how languages work from Lev and his colleagues, build an understanding of interpretation and translation from the world-class staff at MIIS in that area, and study nonproliferation from the international policy experts at a center run by the institute. These were the skills we told their parents and teachers about in Monument Valley.

This combination of skills made some sense on the surface. While the world had little to fear of weapons of mass destruction originating from the Navajo nation, the kids would be analysts, not language experts. They'd be helping the language experts focus their questions and efforts at deciphering information from a range of countries using dozens of languages. It was not deep knowledge of a language that they held, but their unique skills in pattern recognition. This was the special element of the project that Lev had hit upon. And our work that summer had confirmed their skills at recognizing patterns, as well as their skills at reading people.

The work to prepare for them flew by over a few weeks, as I got acclimated to Monterey and MIIS.

I would stop into the Housing Office from time to time, but never saw Aileen. Finally, I spotted her across campus. I waved and smiled, but neither of us had time to stop and talk.

Then, one day, she came up to me with her laptop in hand.

Aileen smiled as she walked up. "Hey, there! Good to see you. Stefan tells me you can help me install Office?"

"What, I'm sorry…?" I was happy to see her, but confused.

"Stefan? From the language lab?"

"Oh, right." I confirmed.

Stefan was working in Lev's lab this summer too. He had been Lev's student assistant for the past year. He was graduating that fall, so he cut back his work schedule to be able to focus on his final project - the culminating portfolio. Stefan was passing the lab tech torch to me, including apparently sharing lab licenses of software with cute grad students. I didn't need to be asked twice by Aileen.

"So, can you install it for me?" Aileen asked.

Well, maybe I did need to be asked twice.

"Absolutely! Why don't you give me your laptop now, and I'll have it all ready to go in the morning," I said.

"Sorry, no. I can't hand it over. I need to use it this evening. I was hoping you could come over to my place later to do the install."

"Oh…uh. I see. Sure. Where do you live?" I stammered.

"The basement of that blue house on the corner. Come around 7:30," Aileen invited.

"Ok. I'll see you then," I said with a smile on my face.

Aileen was back in my life, like a flash. Talking to her made my heartbeat pick up. I was trained to be aware of my body, and this was a definite change in my mood, focus, and energy. I was also trained in ways to hold off these changes. But, I saw no need to here. Just let things flow and happen naturally. A part of me felt like an adolescent, shy around the new girl I had just met.

I finished my work day, cleaned up at home, then grabbed a quick meal at the natural foods co-op grocery in Pacific Grove. I brought the tech support gear I might need.

I found the blue house, but did not see stairs down to the basement. Just stairs up to the main entrance. It was a huge house, a grand entrance to a massive upstairs. You could envision a time when the friends of a wealthy family spent all their time up the stairs, relaxing and chatting, while a cadre of helpful staff buzzed around in the basement to care for the needs upstairs.

I started up the stairs, but the porch was dark. It didn't seem right. I was a tad early, so I decided to walk around the house and investigate. A great thing I did. As I walked around the side of the house, I could see out back that some stairs led down to what was clearly a basement door. It even had an address number above it, showing it was an apartment. I walked toward the door and my nose was filled with the most pleasant flower bloom - jasmine growing in vines above the doorway. All good signs I had found the right place.

I got nerves and hesitated before ringing the doorbell. No turning back at this point, Rogue, just keep moving ahead. I rang the bell.

"Hello! Great, come on in. Oh, you seem tall."

I had snapped into my old training, kicking in when my body sensed a bit of nerves. I stood tall and at the ready, carrying an air of authority. That's why I seemed taller.

"Well, I did eat my spinach this evening."

She giggled politely. I'd have to do better with the humor later in the evening.

A new scent filled my nose - warm and chocolate, something was in the oven.

"In a few minutes the bars will be ready. You do like bars, right?"

What was she saying about "bars"? I had no idea. "Yep. Love them! That would be great." Fingers crossed.

I got to work on the laptop doing the installation. She had a nice, newer Apple laptop. I was just lucky to have had my dad's old portable PC. It was just good enough to run a simple word processor and draft papers for class. I then always had to use the computer lab to finalize my work and print it or submit it. Her machine in comparison was like a Cadillac of computing.

"Nice Mac!" I said.

"Thanks! My grandmother bought it for me when I started school. She lives up in San Jose."

As I got Office doing it's thing, she walked in from the kitchen. "Here's a bit of coffee and a bar for you."

We sat down to chat while the machine churned away. The bar was like a brownie or more like a blondie, with a cookie dough base, chocolate chips, caramel, nuts and such on top. It tasted great and went really well with the fresh coffee.

"So, I have to admit, I've never heard of 'bars' as a desert treat. This one is great, but..."

"Oh yeah, 'bars.' I guess that's a Minnesota term. Any flat cookie type thing baked in a pan, then cut into bar shapes. Lemon bars, brownies, blondies, and such. We have hundreds of recipes for bars where I come from."

"Aha. Like I said, this one is great!"

"I'm glad you like it, I'm sending you home with another dozen. As a thank you for the computer work." She smiled.

I smiled back as our eyes met. At that moment the laptop beeped at us, indicating it was done with the installation work. I looked away, coughed, and went back to the machine.

"Yep, it's all done. Here it is, open and ready for your next paper!"

She smiled and sat down, typing away to test it out. "Thank you so much!"

I sat back, finished my bar, and had some coffee. As much as I was relaxed and enjoying myself, I suddenly got a wave of shy panic. I just couldn't stay there any longer.

"Well, ... I ... uh ... actually need to get going," I stammered as I stood up.

She snapped out of her typing focus, turned around, a hint of disappointment on her face. Then she smiled and said, "Wait!"

That got my attention. I paused and looked up at her. She met my eyes, looking back. I smiled. After a moment, she headed to the kitchen. "I've got those bars for you. Here they are."

She brought them out and handed them to me. I smiled as I looked at the bars wrapped in foil. As I took them from her, our hands made contact - her touch was warm, there was something electric. I looked up straight into her eyes. Eventually, our hands pulled away from each other.

I gave a shy smile, then said, "These are great. Thank you so much."

"No. Thank you! The bars are nothing. I really don't know how to thank you enough..."

In the doorway, as I turned around one more time to look, there was a softness in her eyes. I didn't want to leave.

"I, uh, ... really want to kiss you." The words came out of my mouth.

She leaned in, grabbed my shirt and pulled me in for a kiss. I closed my eyes and melted into the kiss. Her lips were soft and warm. There was a warmth that traveled through me, lit me up from the inside the way the rocks lit up in the Monument Valley sunset. I was energized and I took the kiss deeper, finding a welcome response from Aileen.

It seemed to last all evening, but I'm sure it was no more than 5 seconds. We released from the kiss, looking into each other's eyes.

"Wow," I said. Nothing more came out.

She smiled and said, "Wow!" right back at me.

"So, what was I saying? Oh yeah, I need to get going."

She just looked at me.

"Ok, so need is not the right word. Ah, shoot, I don't need to do anything, except spend the evening hanging out with you."

We both laughed.

"Let's go get some coffee," I said. And we headed out.

Chapter Eleven

NAVAJOS IN MONTEREY

The day before the kids arrived, Lev and I put a few final pieces together. They were registered for introductory linguistics and a translation and interpretation class. The point was not to become language teaching experts, but to learn enough about how language systems work that they could analyze data coming in from different language sources. The point was also not to become interpreters or translators, but to tap into some of those skills that stretch the brain to be able to track two linguistic systems at once.

Maybe one of the kids would want to go further with interpreting, and that would be great. They were already bilingual in Navajo and English. If they wanted to master a third or fourth language for interpretation purposes that would be fine - it would help the project. It wouldn't be anything they did in the first year or two, but they could certainly get a start. They also took a few policy courses related to non-proliferation.

In some ways, their schedules were wacky - they were non-traditional students. But, enough students at MIIS made their own course of study that they wouldn't stand out. And, generally, if someone started to stand out, most of the students knew not to ask too many questions.

We had setup a workroom for them off the lab. There were a number of spaces set aside as offices, so we converted one, providing three of the latest high power laptops for them to use as primary stations to do their homework, and start to learn their analysis tools.

Lev had pulled together a server with a number of useful concordances, the linguistic analysis tool they would become experts in. He showed me around them. The queries and connections one could make with such a tool were fascinating. Used for study of the bible for years, these tools were now focused on large databases of naturally occurring language samples. These tools form a direct technological link to the large language models paired up with reinforcement learning that power generative AI systems.

Concordances allow superb analysis of patterns and usage in language. Lev had even connected with a researcher in Flagstaff who had spent years collecting and cataloging Navajo language samples. We had loaded this Navajo database into the concordance tool, ready for some digging and exploration by our scholarship winners.

"I think we may be ready, Lev. I'm sure some new things will come up, but this is a great foundation to jump start the training of these three kids."

"Sure. You are right. We can make adjustments as we go. I think it's time for a beer to celebrate!" Lev said this assuredly as more of a command than an invitation.

"Lev, thanks. You know I love sitting down over a beer with you. But, I actually have some other plans." I used a gentle tone to create a soft opening instead of a forceful pushback against his command.

Lev was puzzled at first, his head so deep into our work together. "What? Oh... yeah. Of course. Give my best to Aileen!" He smiled supportively as he said those final words. Lev had Aileen in a number of classes, knew her well, and respected her understanding of language teaching. He was happy to see the two of us youngsters find each other.

We went to dinner in New Monterey. This was our first evening out together, not counting the software installation, or grabbing a burrito over lunch. I wanted to spend time with her before the students arrived, when I knew the pace of life would take off.

We shared an appetizer. I let her taste my soup. I got my standard veggie burger, while she went for a more sophisticated, but earthy entree.

"Do you want to try a bite of my burger?" I asked as I sliced off a clean corner piece for her to sample.

Aileen said, "Sure!" and had a bite. We had already broken that comfort barrier where you could share food off your plate and not feel like you were intruding on someone else. The bite she gave me of her squash entree was tasty and a bit surprising.

The waitress came by, asking if we wanted desert or coffee. I was in the mood for tea, but had a question.

"This tea here. Is it Peppermint Sleepy Time?"

"It's two teas. Peppermint, or Sleepy Time," the waitress clarified.

"That's what I thought, but I didn't see a comma. I'll have a cup of Peppermint please. Do you want anything Aileen?" I asked and turned to my date.

As I looked over, she was suppressing a laugh. "Let's share a piece of apple pie?"

The next morning, the Greyhound bus arrived with Alice, Earl, and Jason. Lev and I met them there and walked with them up to the Defense Language Institute. The students would be housed in this military facility located on the Monterey Presidio. They would spend their days learning a military style regimen, mixing with a bunch of young military linguists.

The linguists had gone through basic training and been identified as having talents related to language learning and applications of language skills. They came to the DLI for intensive instruction in strategic languages like Arabic, Chinese, Russian, Korean, Spanish. Along with months of rigorous language acquisition work, they also learned techniques of listening and transcribing. These linguists operated as the ears of our military and government. Once they graduated, they would be posted in areas where they could intercept communications from within the borders of our foreign adversaries. It was their job to catch those transmissions and quickly make sense of them. Others would analyze the translated information in their reports, but these linguists were the first step in an important intelligence gathering net.

Living and training alongside the military linguists would provide the Navajo students a sense of teamwork, but also a view on how linguists swept up relevant information, and how they fine tuned their language skills for intelligence gathering.

"We have to live here?" Alice was unimpressed with the barracks.

"Well, this one is the men's barracks." I responded. "The women's one is similar - perhaps a bit more cared for on the inside. You'll get to really like it. The other trainees here are fascinating young people!"

"I think most days we'll be so tired we aren't going to care where we lay down," said Jason. He seemed to know what they were in for, but he was also quite motivated to be here, after fighting so hard for the opportunity.

Once they dropped off their stuff, Lev and I took the kids on a tour of the peninsula. We started near the Institute and the DLI, showing where to find bagels or a movie on a weekend. We drove them past a few grocery stores so they could see the range of options. We showed them some of the beautiful scenery along the 17 mile drive, and into quaint Carmel. We wrapped up by bringing them to a nice meal on Fisherman's Wharf. The seafood was fresh and varied, the setting was sophisticated, not cheap, the kids relaxed and ate well.

The next morning, Earl and the other two reported to the lab at 10am. They had already done a 2 mile run, had breakfast, and been given a tour of the Presidio. Lev gave them a chance to check in, asking what they knew of the project and how they felt about it.

"This is what I signed up for," said Jason. "I'm ready to learn as much as I can."

"Can you explain what this will be doing for the country? Once we are trained?" Asked Alice.

Lev answered, "You will be keeping nuclear weapons and other nasty tools out of the hands of the real bad guys - crazy, unpredictable actors on the world stage."

Jason's eyes bugged out a bit when he heard that. He knew they had been singled out, but this task seemed really important. He wanted to learn everything he could - to do his best in this role.

Alice scrunched up her forehead. "That's quite a claim. You want us to believe a couple of kids from Monument Valley can do that?"

"I know you can," I said. "Not this moment, of course. You need training. That's why you are here."

"Then we should get started. What's up first?" Earl stepped in to nudge things forward, maybe help Alice focus back on their work.

"Concordances!" Lev exclaimed. "This is the first tool you will need. A concordance will help you make connections between two disparate samples of language. Type in an idiom and see what comes up."

Alice spoke up first. "I typed in 'ball and chain,' and it listed 30 instances of the phrase. What does that mean?"

"You have to look at those 30 instances, the 30 places it was used. See how it is used, what language goes around it. What patterns can you see?"

The kids were drawn in as Lev got into deep explanation mode.

"So, here the phrase is used by an anonymous source talking to the main political reporter for the biggest newspaper in Tel Aviv, Israel. If we look at other places where that phrase is used in the Israeli press, we see two other instances of an anonymous source talking to that same reporter. Perhaps this is the same person talking repeatedly to the same reporter. Then, we find someone using that phrase in a news article, but their name is used - Freddy Perlman - we might be able to guess that Perlman is the anonymous source."

"Sounds like a wild guess?" exclaimed Earl.

"And 'ball and chain' is a pretty common phrase." Alice chimed in as well. "What are the odds this is two, or even three or four different people?"

"Ok. All good points. Those are questions you need to be asking. To be honest, I don't know the odds. But, I want you all to be able to tell me that eventually. You will have lots of time to play with these tools to get used to the types of answers you can find. Let's keep digging into this one. How could we make it less of a wild guess, Earl?"

Alice jumped in for Earl. "We can look at what this Perlman says in the article and try to find other matches to stories from that Tel Aviv reporter."

"Precisely! See what you can find. One tip. We started with an idiom. You can use other short phrases that are not well known. There's something called collocation in linguistics. This is a set of words that are often found together. They are not as strong as idioms where they have a special meaning when used together. It's just a common clustering of words. Like 'down on the farm'. The phrase 'on the farm', or 'on my farm', or even 'at the farm' would work just fine, but for some reason people use 'down on the farm' a lot together. That's a collocation. You could say idioms are special forms of collocations. Well, this Perlman has his own style of phrasing that uses certain collocations more than others, or more than other people would use them. It's part of what makes up a person's style of speaking. Think of someone you know who has a unique style of speaking."

"My uncle Jim," said Earl.

Alice and Jason laughed. They knew Uncle Jim too. He was a colorful character, loved to talk anyone's ear off.

Earl went on, "Uncle Jim runs a souvenir shop on the reservation selling rugs, baskets, bead work. When tourists come in, he has a thousand stories to tell them. He draws people into the stories - something about the way he talks - you know you are listening to an Uncle Jim story. People from around the world come in and say, 'My cousin was here last summer and told me I need to stop in to see Uncle Jim.' Man, he does great business."

"Ok, so imagine you are listening to your Uncle Jim tell one of his stories, can you think of a collocation he uses? Something that makes it sound like an Uncle Jim story."

"Up on that mesa over there!" Alice and Jason laughed, shaking their heads up and down.

Earl continued, "Every story he tells happened on a nearby mesa, according to Uncle Jim. Even when they really happened a hundred miles away in another part of the Navajo nation. He still tells it like it happened right in sight of his shop, or wherever he is. Then these poor German tourists walk out, take a picture of the mesa and bring it home to tell their friends what happened 'up on that mesa over there.'"

"Perfect. Great example. When you hear Uncle Jim tell a story, that collocation helps you know who you are listening to. And

Freddy Perlman has his own 'up on that mesa over there.' Or dozens of them. So, use that to try to find more matches between his public statements and this anonymous source for our friend in Tel Aviv. This database has every news article on weapons systems in the Israeli media for the past 15 years. It also has all public government documents, transcribed speeches from officials and the like from Israel and neighboring countries. So, if Mr. Perlman helped form policy and contributed to any of those documents, you may find more of his typical speech patterns. More ways to test whether he is that anonymous source for our reporter friend."

Alice had another quizzical look. "Was all of this published in English? That's a ton of material."

"Heh. Another important point. No, most of this was not published in English. It originated in Hebrew. You are working with translated data sets here. At MIIS our Center for Non-proliferation Studies does yeoman's work gathering up this data, translating it, cleaning it up. They have some peers in other countries and we share data sets. But, years ago, the Center's director put forward this claim that public documents and media could be a powerful tool to understanding what different countries were doing. He focused his attention on his pet issue - the spread of weapons of mass destruction around the globe. Boy, was he right. His analysis and analysts from his teams have helped numerous US efforts in stopping and reversing proliferation, as well as efforts by our allies."

"So, then why are we here?" asked Jason.

"You three have the chance to bring this effort to the next level." Lev paused, looking at each of their faces. "To get our analysis closer to real time findings. To catch interactions between bad players as they happen, or are about to happen, rather than months later. You have just the right set of skills. And with our training here in linguistics, translation, intelligence approaches, and other bits, you will be quite a team!"

Jason looked over at Earl, and then to Alice. They all had a look of pride, but also concern on their faces. The three of them? How could they be so special?

Chapter Twelve

NAVY TRAINING

Jason and Earl came back from their morning run to head to hand-to-hand training.

"Jason, line up with Earl over there!"

"Yes, Major!" Jason replied. His voice was firm and confident, but the look on his face was muddled. I had come by to see how the training was going for the recruits. The major had resisted my request to have them face off. But, it was an important exercise for a number of reasons.

Earl stepped up in ready stance. All three recruits had been through 3 months of combat training. They were young and active. They could hold their own.

"Men, get yourselves in position. You will spar for 2 minutes - I want to see everything you've been learning here," the major gave his directions.

Jason cleared his mind, used the breathing techniques they had all learned to quickly move from being at rest to being ready to pounce. He, too, was ready.

A whistle blew. Earl jumped right into action, coming forward strong with a one-two thrust of his fists. Jason stepped back and to his left, leaving Earl to slightly stumble a bit off center. Jason watched as Earl recovered, favoring his left leg for balance. They both had learned something about their opponent.

Jason let Earl turn around and gain his ground, then immediately came in with a sweeping kick toward that left leg. As Earl evaded, it was a glancing blow, not a solid hit. But, Jason was sounding out his route of attack.

Earl rolled right around to bring his hand down from overhead on Jason's back. Jason stumbled forward, off center, putting one hand down before popping back up. That was Earl warning Jason that he was not taking this lightly.

I could see a bit of anger well up inside Jason. Maybe he didn't want Earl to embarrass him in front of the other trainees. Jason had told me about Earl back in Monument Valley. He and Earl had never been rivals in school, but they were also not best buddies. Jason told stories about some old tension between their fathers. So, while he treated Earl respectfully at school and in their Monterey training, I imagine he always carried a bit of a suspicion about Earl, wondering if he had the same character flaws Jason's dad had described about Earl's dad.

Earl came in again, thrusting toward Jason, trying to build on the impact he had had on Jason's back. This time, anticipating Jason going back and to the left, he thrusted forward with a single punch, then swept his right leg around from his right to catch Jason as he moved to the left.

Jason got knocked off his feet by this move. The major recorded a point for Earl in the sparring bout. It was best two out of three. Jason needed to score the next point or it would be over.

The boys had a few seconds to stand up, take a breath and get back in ready position. Earl was there, ready again, right away. Jason took a second to shake off the kick to his leg, take a breath, then re-focus and come into ready position in the center.

This time, Jason jumped forward right away to get things moving. He swept his leg around high at Earl's head, then spun around as Earl backed up and did a one-two punch toward Earl's chest. Earl kept backing up. Jason had learned that Earl would favor his left leg for balance, as he'd done before, so he kept the pressure on Earl, pushing him toward his right foot, with rapid fire kicks and punches. In the end, he didn't land any of them - I don't think he meant to land any of them. But, in quick succession, he got Earl to stumble backward on that weaker right leg and roll out of the ring. A whistle blew and the major scored a point for Jason.

Earl seemed a bit winded and taken aback. Now he knew Jason was not backing down. Earl had always acted like he was a bit superior to Jason, both in Monument Valley and then in Monterey during training as well. I had seen Jason act a bit deferentially to Earl, not challenging him directly, giving him some space in classes and with projects.

Jason gave Earl a bit of breathing room, he didn't line up at the ready right away. Earl shook off the fall, looked around, and caught his breath. He was ready for this and stepped up at the ready in the center of the sparring ring. Jason came in right away, like he didn't want Earl to be too comfortable up front.

I caught the major's eye and waved a signal at him. The major stepped up and grabbed the right hand of each boy.

"Alright!" The boys both looked surprised, were a bit off balance. Could it have been two minutes already? "That's it, boys. Save that energy and enthusiasm for today's new drills."

Both boys stepped back a bit stunned. Perhaps a bit relieved as well. They had unfinished business, certainly. But, I was hoping they didn't want to push so hard as to ruin their working relationship.

"Guys, nice match!" I approached the young men.

"Anthony, what are you doing here?"

"Watching you guys. I remember having a bout like that with one of my early partners. Helped me get to know him better, know what he was capable of."

"When do I get to spar these chumps?" asked Alice.

"I'm sure it will be a round robin," I smiled. "Once you are cleaned up, I'm bringing you three to the Naval Postgraduate School."

"Postgraduate what?" Earl asked. "We have barely begun, more or less graduated. How can we be post-graduates already."

"Look. The name is mostly descriptive. Sure, the typical officer who comes to NPS has a degree or two already. But, the real focus of the school is on analysis techniques. The students are all intelligence officers," I explained.

"Intelligence? I thought we were learning about that from the DLI gang. How they get trained in for listening posts, language skills, transcription, and all that." Earl was the inquisitive one today.

"That's intelligence gathering," I answered. "You need to understand that, certainly. And you need to understand the language skills the linguists gain while they are here at the DLI."

"How about all this running and combat training?" Earl fired off another question.

"Earl, yes, even that will be highly valuable to you three. As will the discipline you are gaining from the major and others on the base. Plus, all the relationships you are making with individual linguists will be useful down the road, too, I'm sure."

"But you were telling us about the post-graduate school." Jason brought me back on track.

"Right. The officers who train at NPS are analysts. They don't listen and transcribe. They pull together a file of information and make sense of it. They provide summaries of large sets of intelligence." I carried on in tutor mode. "They provide suggestions and advice to their superiors - you will be providing advice to your superiors. Analysis will be the task you perform most often."

"We're already doing that with the concordance work," Alice said with confidence. "It's the best part of our training so far."

"Alice, that is music to my ears. These NPS guys are the best in the world. You will learn so much from them." I was really talking up this new phase.

The students got ready and we headed out. We drove out of the Presidio, along the edge of downtown right by the ocean, and headed east toward Seaside.

Just before leaving Monterey, a gated facility popped up to our right. There was a guard post just off Del Monte Boulevard. No one was allowed to accidentally turn in here.

We parked inside the facility, along our way to the library at the center of the property. We were met at the entrance by Lt. Carney. Carney had a everyday kind of guy look - someone who could fade into a crowd unnoticed. He walked up to us with a confident stride that said, "Navy-trained" with every step. I introduced him to the kids.

"Alice, Earl, Jason... This is Lt. Jim Carney. He will be your primary instructor at NPS. He is in charge of this whole school, but has taken you on as his special assignment. You are in good hands."

I shared this with the students to make sure they understood the value of this part of their learning.

"Anthony! Thanks so much. Kids, you are lucky to be working with this young man, Mr. Rogue. I hope you are paying attention to him. I've known Anthony since we were in training together in the '80's and he will always have your back."

Jim didn't go into the story illustrating how important it was that I did have his back - that would have to wait for another day. I said farewell to the young recruits, leaving them in Jim's expert hands.

That evening, Alice came to me privately to express her concern.

"Lt. Carney is not teaching us much, Mr. Rogue."

"Call me Anthony. We are colleagues now."

She smiled nervously. "Anthony...? We were just playing word games all day."

"And what were you expecting?" I asked.

"Training in analysis. That's what this place is supposed to be all about. I was expecting some scenarios and simulations. I mean..."

I cut her off. "So impatient. The so called word games are puzzles of a sort, right?"

She nodded.

"This is the start of the training. Carney is stripping things down a bit, getting a start..."

It was her turn to interrupt. "We don't need to be babied. I mean, we were brought here because of our natural abilities and special talents, right?" She was pausing for affirmation, but in a rhetorical sense. She knew the answer.

"Right, that's true." I was giving a clear signal to go on.

"So, why waste our time with kid stuff?" Showing a bit of anger now.

"Ok, I hear you. You are not being babied. Here's the scoop. Lt. Carney knows his stuff. He knows what you all are capable of. He has diagnosed some needs, he's stripping things down as I said earlier. His approach, which has been working for hundreds of analysts over the years, will show results for you guys too. I know we have put you through some accelerated paces since you've arrived in Monterey. The pace of this too will pick up. I promise you will not be bored. And what Carney is working on now will make you a better analyst. You will see the fruits, and I will even go so far as to say you will be amazed."

She gave me a long, hard look, like she was considering where to go next in the conversation. I wondered if she was ever amazed by her own skills. The intense look in her eyes receded, then her jaw and shoulders relaxed a bit. Finally, a soft smile began to emerge as she let her anxiety fade.

"Ok. I'll be patient. I'm ready for Lt. Carney to amaze me." With that she bid me goodnight and headed back to the DLI for the night.

I called up Aileen to see if she had time for an evening stroll by the water. I needed a break from the stresses of the project. I enjoyed talking with her. She seemed to understand me, she listened generously. Aileen was free that night and was happy to get a breath of fresh air.

I really wanted to tell Aileen all about these kids and what their real purpose was in town.

Aileen had met Alice and the boys, and she seemed to like them. She knew they had a specially designed program involving collaboration between MIIS and the DLI. But, the details and depth of the project could not be shared. An Agent knows where that dividing line is between what can be shared and what needs to be held back. That night, I would just turn on that switch, and enjoy our time together otherwise.

Monterey was such a beautiful area to take an evening stroll. Comfortable temperatures. Cool enough to wear a fleece, but not chilly enough to be inhospitable. Clear views over the bay - boats, the wharf, the smell of the ocean. You could hear the water breaking on a beach, or up against a wall built up along the shore. There were sea lions barking in the distance, birds overhead.

Holding Aileen's hand, listening to stories from her, talking about languages and language teaching, discussing music and travel. It was all so comfortable and felt right. I had never been more at peace than when I spent time with her by the water in Monterey.

Chapter Thirteen

A BOND EVOLVES

"Hal, I need to talk with someone about this. I just can't keep it inside anymore."

"Anthony, thanks for calling me. Sounds like quite a dilemma. I'm always happy to be a sounding board, a confidant. Tell me the story." Hal's voice was a welcome source of support.

"I met her when I first arrived in Monterey. Aileen is amazing. We meet women in this field - always traveling, always creating new facets of our assumed identity. With our understandable air of mystery, women are often drawn in. It's easy to connect with someone briefly, have some fun, and move on. That's what our lifestyle is built for. And, yet, that is not what is happening right now."

"Tell me about Aileen." Hal was listening.

"She has this smile. It is natural and effortless. When I see her smile, it makes me smile. I find myself wanting to make her smile. Her eyes are beautiful and warm. I look into them and I feel safe. I feel ... loved. I'm sorry, there's no other word. I don't normally talk like this, Hal. But, I really can't say it any other way. When we walk around Monterey and talk about life, classes, her travels to Scotland or wherever, my years at Caltech, whatever, it just feels so comfortable. Our view of the world lines up. We love some of the same music - I'm not just talking about big name groups like U2, but obscure stuff like the Notting Hillbillies or Peter Himmelman. I can't deny that she and I connect... And....I.... I am in love with her."

"Have you told her that?"

"No, I haven't."

"That's good." Hal said definitively.

"I thought so too. But you know what? With other women, one's I didn't care about, I'd say the words, no problem. I knew they wanted to hear it. I knew I'd be moving on. So, I wanted them to feel good. I'd say the words."

"So, why haven't you used them with Aileen?" Hal was genuinely curious.

"I am afraid to admit it to myself. Saying it out loud will make it real. Once it is real, I don't know if I can step back. I love her, Hal. I want to spend my life with her."

"Anthony, we don't get to do that. You know that, right?"

"What do you mean?"

"It's the You Only Live Twice rule."

"Are you talking about James Bond?"

"Yep, Anthony. That's the book where Bond gets married. You've read it, right?"

"Please, of course, Hal."

"So, Bond gets married, remember? And he heads off for a honeymoon with his wife."

"But, the bad guys follow him, that's right." I say with a sudden realization. "He's driving on a roadway with her next to him, joking and laughing."

"Yep, then they shoot her. Dead, on the spot. Bond pulls over, but there is nothing he can do for her. She's gone. The one good thing in his life is ripped away."

"Gosh, right, Hal, I remember. He blames himself. Had he let her go, like all the others, they would know she didn't mean anything. But, they figured they could injure him forever. Take him out of the game. It almost worked too. He laid low for a year or two, but then he came back with a vengeance."

"The You Only Live Twice rule. You can't get married and stay in the Agency - in the field. If you do it, you retire and move on to another career. Or, you end the relationship like all the others. And get back to the work you are trained for."

"But, Bond is just a fictitious character. The Agency can't really base a rule on a storybook hero. And a British one at that!"

Hal laughed at that last bit, a dig at our friends across the pond. "The books may be fiction, Anthony, but Ian Fleming knew his way around the field, my friend. It's easy to forget, watching the almost comic book zaniness of some of the modern Bond films. But those books from the Sixties had some authenticity to them. That's what made them such a success. Like some of Tom Clancy's early work. He knew his material."

"Hal...what should I do? I feel like a part of me is dying. If I leave the Agency, I don't know what I will do. Who is Anthony Rogue outside the Agency? Anthony Rogue would be dead! But, I can't live without Aileen. She is all I care about in the end. How can I leave her behind? How can I break up with her, cause her that kind of pain, and still live with myself? How can I lie that deeply? I love her... Hal, I love her."

"I am not you, Anthony. I can't make that choice. You have to decide it for yourself. You can do it."

"Hal...I've never done anything this hard in my life."

The next week was Valentine's Day. I made a date with Aileen, asking her to dress up a bit fancy. I tried to do the same. Neither one of us had really fancy clothes with us in Monterey. She cleaned up really well though. No need to put on a classic Dior gown like celebrities wear on the red carpet; she can turn heads around town in much simpler clothes.

Aileen wore a simple black dress, that hugged her hips and showed off her curves. It was medium length, showing enough of her legs to display how fit she was, riding her bike or roller blading along the coastline five or six times a week. Her skin was healthy and vibrant, reflecting the way she ate well, buying fresh produce at the weekly farmer's market, staying away from fast food, eating whole foods, and cooking from scratch more often than not.

All this to say she was beautiful and radiant that night. A knockout!

I led her toward downtown, taking a path we often walked, headed to a coffee house or a taqueria for lunch. On our way, we always walked past Mon Trio, a nationally known, formal, and upscale restaurant. Looking in the window, we always expected to see local celebrities like Clint Eastwood or Hollywood stars like John Travolta. We walked past and looked in the window. She looked at me as we continued walking. I reached down to hold her hand, then I slowed, grabbed her hand tighter and led her around, making in a counter-clockwise half turn to head back to the restaurant.

We walked right up to the door, I held it open for her, and the hostess said, "Mr. Rogue, you are right on time. Your table is waiting for you." I couldn't help myself, my eyes lit up as I grinned ear to ear. I could see the excitement in her face, even as she was walking by me into the restaurant.

We sat down and just soaked in the atmosphere. This was not a restaurant for university students. Tonight, we left behind those identities. We were treating ourselves, I was treating her, to an extravagance.

When the waiter came for our order, I let her speak up. "I'd like the seared scallops, the organic greens, and a small glass of local Chardonnay."

"And for you, sir?"

"I'd love the mushroom risotto and a bowl of tomato basil soup, with Perrier and lime."

We shared bites of our meals, then ordered a chocolate cake to split. I asked for a coffee and she ordered a black tea with milk and a bit of sugar. While we waited for the dessert, they cleared our other plates.

I reached out my hand across the table and looked in her eyes. She took my hand and smiled.

"Aileen, this has been a great night. Happy Valentine's Day."

She blushed a bit and was about to reply. Then I said those words.

"Aileen, I love you."

She was silenced, taken aback. She was clearly pleased to hear how I felt, but didn't respond immediately.

They brought our dessert and drinks at that point, so we let go of each other's hands.

As they walked away, she stood up a bit and leaned forward. She got up close to my left ear, I could feel her warmth, and she whispered in my ear, "Me too."

As she said it, a tear welled up in my right eye, and trailed down my cheek. That ear to ear grin appeared once again.

That was the best chocolate cake and richest coffee I have ever tasted in my life. As I walked her home, I was floating like a cumulus cloud high above the earth.

I had figured it out. I knew what I was going to do. I needed to take an action. The timing was not right that night. But, when it was, I knew what path I was going to take. It had been the hardest decision in my life. But, I knew I had gotten it right. I was doing the right thing.

Chapter Fourteen

THE FINAL PIECES

We were coming to the final stage of developing these recruits. They had flown along with every challenge we had given them. Lev and I worked with them a few times a week in their workroom. Lev pulled up unique concordance data, I would pose some questions from real world situations happening around the globe, and we would put them to work.

Sometimes Alice took the lead, sometimes Earl. Jason always started down his own path of discovery, trying creative approaches.

"So, here's the heart of the matter," Earl said. "The terrorist leader went underground 6 weeks ago. Somewhere in the data there must be a trail of his that goes cold."

"He gave an interview to Al Jazeera 2 months ago, and they said he was in Beirut," Alice jumped in.

"Ok, I'll look at that interview and pick out some of his collocations to see where else his vocal tell signs appear." Earl was taking the lead. Alice was following a similar path alongside him to check his conclusions and scour the data faster. Earl asked, "Jason, are you with us?"

"Never mind him," Alice said. "He's got his own pet theory he's busy eliminating. He'll circle back in due time."

A few minutes later, Jason piped up. "Arabic has dozens of dialects. Al Jazeera's Arabic to English translator is from Yemen, using an Arabian peninsula dialect. But, this terrorist leader comes from the mountains of Morocco. For general news, most of the translations from Al Jazeera are pretty faithful. But, most mainstream Arabic speakers find this mountain dialect from Morocco to be offensive to the ear. The translator can't help but clean it up."

"Ok, where are you going, wild man?" Earl smiled, realizing Jason was on to something.

"So, I took some of the snippets from that interview and dirtied them up with an Arabic reference Professor Fahad gave us a few weeks back. When I search using more colloquial forms of his words from the news report, I find some matches in a document from last week. It's a press release from a local Al Qaeda affiliate in Eastern Egypt. The group is known as almost 100% Egyptian. There is no way any of them would be caught dead using Arabic like that."

Alice finished the thought, "So our underground terrorist has emerged in Eastern Egypt, running the show there. Great work, Jason. Let's see what other data we can dig up about this cell and get it all over to the Agency."

I was duly impressed with this exercise. We had truly lost track of this guy, and their efforts ended up getting us back on his tail, so we could continue to keep the pressure on.

It was time to bring in the big data sets from the Center for Non-proliferation Studies. We had collated and cleansed the data used in the training for our Navajo all stars thus far. Now, they seemed ready for a raw, comprehensive data set straight from the Center.

The Center had servers on the network where they stored all the documents they had collected, catalogued, and translated. They were always expanding the SAN, increasing the storage capacity. There were documents related to all the players in the Middle East, North Korea, Russia, many former Soviet Republics, China, India, Pakistan, Cuba, and various bad actors in Africa and South America. Every set of documents expanded each week. With local students driving immediate growth and international partners providing mountains of additional data, the Center seemed to double its database size every 4-6 months.

The Center was running into a problem where no outside analysts were able to delve into the information they had collected. Some of the students who had worked through the document collecting and cataloging could still find and access complex sets of data they had helped build. But, the real benefit of the collection process was in providing tools and analysis to support the needs of dozens of intelligence agencies around the globe.

We had the analysts to do the work, but now we needed one final element to bring the puzzle together - visual tools to support the modeling of these large, naturalistic data sets.

I brought in some old friends from my Caltech days who were now well ensconced in Silicon Valley, at all the big firms. But, there was one fellow in particular, who had built the AdvertMap technology at the core of the business model over at SearchBot, the search engine king. Evan Leavy - I asked him to support the project and he was happy to help, even if the support had to be kept quiet.

"Kids - let me tell you a bit of background before we dive into the tool I brought for you. I sold my stake in AdvertMap to SearchBot, stayed on as a director for them for a few years, then got the itch. I had a new puzzle to solve. So, I went off with a few engineer buddies to start things up again, this time focused squarely on Big Data. We moved from linguistic analysis to visual analysis. Sure, this new tool we are building leverages linguistics like AdvertMap does, but the key to making sense of it was to move to a mode of communication more efficient in humans. And that is visual data. We call ourselves 1000 Words."

"Ah, like a picture is worth...," said Earl.

"Yep! I brought a beta version of the tool to you. It's got our latest technology in a raw form. Our early testing is promising. I think it suits this project well. So, here we go."

Evan brought up a display on a wall of the lab. It showed clusters of data. "This is one of the Big Data collections from the Center for Nonproliferation Studies," he said. "The clusters represent relationships between data points - based on the linguistic analysis. So, to begin, we can look at this data by location."

As Evan said this, he used hand gestures to interact with the controls along the side of the display. He didn't have to walk up to the wall. He was immersed in the data, between the projector unit and the wall. There must've been an input device that could pick up motion like a game control sensor. Evan turned on a map overlay. Now, the clusters appeared on a map of former Soviet republics.

"As you can see, this data pertains to information sourced out of these various countries. Where do you all want to go?"

"Kazakhstan," shot Jason immediately.

Leavy found it on the map, then used both hands to center attention on it and with a zooming motion of both hands, brought us in close on the map to Kazakhstan.

"As you'd expect, when you zoom, the data re-arranges slightly into clusters within the more detailed locations. Now, here's an interesting question. We've got one big cluster of information coming out of the capital - Astana - makes sense. But, there is a noticeable cluster here, in this border town, Almaty. Let's see what is relevant to both locations."

Leavy used his left hand to pick up the pile of data from the capital, and his right hand to grab the smaller pile from Almaty. As he brought the two piles together in front of him, documents and files started flying back to their original location. The piles in Leavy's hands kept getting smaller, but some items were definitely coming along for the ride.

"So, here I am finding some relevance." Evan said as he held his two hands up next to each other and spun around to show the kids. "It's sort of like a magnet. If these documents have a relationship, they are attracted to each other, or compatible being next to each other. If not, they get pushed back to their origin, set aside."

"Now, I only want the files that really interrelate or interact. Some of the Almaty files must mention Astana and vice versa. That's enough of a relationship to sit side by side." Now, he brought his hands together in a light rubbing motion. "When I push them together like this, only the files that directly reference each other stay, and they start to interact based on this crossing of references."

A smaller set of artifacts stayed in Evan's hands, while a number of files fell away, like skin that had been sloughed off. They fell back to the map, but didn't snap back to their origin.

"These files that fell to the ground might be useful in a minute, so they stick around, just a bit out of focus. The rest, still in my collection, are now clustering based on their interrelation. I can start to pick up a set here or there to find what the topic is, how they are relevant to each other and to my question."

"Let's look at those three pink files over there," Jason was still in charge in this one.

"Ok, cowboy, you come over here and drive," said Evan.

Jason picked up and started examining the documents. Leavy gave him instructions on how to work with 1000 Words. The other Navajo analysts joined in and pretty soon they were getting the hang of it. The tool was even powerful enough that two or three people could be in there manipulating the display and relationships at the same time. You had to be somewhat coordinated with each other, but it could work.

"So, in the same way we used geography and a map to begin our analysis, you can use people, a timeline, and so many other intuitive categories to begin to cluster and analyze these data sets. Tomorrow, we'll have a session where I show you how to put multiple analysis layers over the same data set. For now, I think it's time for a round of well-deserved beers!"

ARROYO SECO

When we headed out that day, I didn't know Aileen was going to save my life. How could I know. She didn't know either of course. It was just a typical weekend day, a day we'd decided to go for a hike with one of her good friends. But, it is a day that now sticks out in our memories, a day that carries major weight in the story arc – the mythology - of our relationship.

Aileen lived in a beautiful part of the country, a beautiful part of the world - Monterey, CA. And I was lucky to be there for awhile on this project. Monterey sits along the Pacific coast, just south of the San Francisco area, at the bottom end of a bay with such beauty and diverse marine life that it warrants a national marine sanctuary designation. And Monterey is just north of Big Sur, a long stretch of dramatic shoreline and parkland that could draw in any nature-lover. Even people who have never been to Big Sur know the imagery well, because it is used in umpteen TV commercials. Anytime you see a car driving along a narrow oceanside highway, taking sharp turns with a craggy coastline or crossing a dramatic, arching bridge over a short but steep drop down to the sea, that's Big Sur. I felt lucky to be posted in Monterey, to have met a wonderful woman like Aileen there, taking bike rides along the mellower, developed coastline near Monterey itself.

Monterey was walkable / bike-able enough to get by fine most days without a car. Sure, a few hills presented a challenge, or carting groceries home did, especially if one of your favorite stores was up one of those challenging hills. But, the weekly farmer's market a few blocks from the campus helped alleviate some of that concern. Buses were something of an option for getting to and from the mall or for the occasional big shopping run. But, by and large, the transportation system did not make it easy to be carless. As much as many folks at the school would've appreciated or expected a European-style transit system with connections easy and often to places not too far away, the students were living in California, alas, where the car is king.

The most tantalizing, but hardest place to get to without a car was Big Sur. It was really not that far away, but biking the distance up and down truly significant hills was more like training for the Tour de France than enjoying a casual day outdoors. And buses certainly went along the coast, but their frequency was so low it made it a really frightening prospect to maybe miss the one trip home you could count on. So, students often went there only in other people's cars. It was a popular destination when people came to visit from out of town and had rental cars. You would did this partly to show the visitor a beautiful location in the area and partly to just spend time there as a local resident.

The day Aileen saved my life we were going on a hiking trip inland from Big Sur. At the north end of this long, dramatic stretch of California coastline is the Carmel Valley, a lush, fertile area with vineyards, organic farms and artists. We were driving into Carmel

Valley to a place called Arroyo Seco. Our opportunity to visit Arroyo Seco came via Aileen's friend named Kelly.

Kelly and Aileen met each other their first year at school, before I was in town. They bonded quickly as two Minnesotans who had come to Monterey for their education. I got to know Kelly after I met Aileen, but she and I had a good bond as well, and probably would've been friends even had we not had Aileen as a common point for meeting each other.

So, Kelly was interested in going on a hike – she'd heard about Arroyo Seco, where one could park a car, then walk down to a calm river for swimming in the midst of beautiful California scenery. She approached Aileen and me to see if we wanted to spend Saturday exploring Arroyo Seco and I gladly said,"Yes." Lucky for me, Aileen said "Yes" too.

If I had to predict a near death experience occurring that day, I would've bet on it being something to do with Kelly's driving. She's a competent driver who is not prone to accidents, as I've known her. But, she is also much more loose and free than Aileen and I would be. Driving along these mountainous roads, with steep drop offs on one side or the other, I am the kind of driver to keep two hands on the wheel at 10 o'clock and 2 o'clock never letting my eyes wander off the road. I'll proudly wear the label of nervous nelly.

Kelly, on the other hand is the type of driver who seems to be looking more at the other people in the car amidst lively discussion than she does seem to be watching the road. She is also a one-handed driver. Picture those iconic sharp curves and steep drop-offs to the sea from the TV commercials. Then add a driver in the vehicle with her head cranked all the way to the backseat and her right hand diving deep into a bag of snack chips to grab some crumbs at the bottom. That was Kelly. Aileen and I were the two white-knuckled, ghostlike figures in the seats around her, eyes glued to the road ahead and mouths agape in silent horror like Munch's The Scream. Now, shove all that into a tiny, 3-cylinder Ford Fiesta that Kelly had bought for $1000 and affectionately dubbed the Half Car. This is how I would have predicted a near death experience that day. But, I'll take away that suspense and tell you now, no car plummeted off the road on this trip.

We found our way to the park and pulled over. There was no park house or map of the trails. Just a parking area with a handful of cars. At one end of the parking area we found a gate through a fence. Kelly did some research before planning to come here. She had been told that you follow the road through the gate, along the mountainside for about a mile where you'll find a trail leading down to the water. At first, we didn't even see the water, so we weren't sure where we were headed. But, we followed the directions and headed out. We saw one set of people coming back with towels on their shoulders and wet hair. We said a friendly hello, but didn't think to ask for advice. Seeing them gave us a clear indication we were headed the right way. Around the bend we could see the river down below. It wasn't that far down, but we clearly weren't there yet.

We weren't seeing any other people. Perhaps we'd have relative privacy once we got to the water - a nice out of the way hike. After awhile, I said, "What about these small paths leading off the main road? Do they lead down to the water?"

"They don't look very well used. I'm pretty certain the path will be really clear," Kelly responded.

"I'm sorry. I'm just getting impatient." After that, I tried to just focus ahead and keep us moving.

We started to hear giggles and laughter from below. People were having a good time in the river and the sounds echoed up the sides of the canyon.

"I'm worried we missed it. It feels like we've been walking more than a mile," Aileen spoke up further down the path. "This main path doesn't seem to be bringing us down the hillside at all."

"I'm starting to feel the same way," answered Kelly. "When will we ever get to the water?"

I saw a path off the main road. This one seemed clearer than the others. "Let's give this a try. If it's not leading to the water, we can always come right back."

The ladies gave it a look. We all checked out where it seemed to lead. Still no one around to ask for advice. Reluctantly, we decided to try it.

Since I was the only one with hiking-type shoes on, I was leading the way on our hike. Feeling confident, I hopped from the main path down a few inch drop onto the ledge just below, noticing as I did that the path headed off to the left. Before fully establishing my footing, I started to spin around to call out to Aileen and Kelly, encouraging them forward. As I did so, my forward momentum carried me just off the edge of that ledge and I slid down, uncertain what was below.

Aileen saw me dropping suddenly and headed my way quickly. I was aware enough to use my arms to grab onto the dirt, the stones, the ledge I had just slid off of. My foot caught on something below me and I stopped, hanging over the side of the ledge.

"Anthony, are you ok?" Aileen called out as she approached.

"Yes," I said hurriedly and in a reassuring way before I even had a chance to assess if I was ok.

"Are your feet on something?" Aileen asked anxiously, hitting a major concern right on the head.

I paused. Good question. "I … don't … know." I let slip out slowly as the realization hit me. In a split second, as I originally came over the ledge, I had looked down. All I could tell was that it was a ways down – nothing just below me. So, how could I be OK, if I didn't know what was keeping me from falling further, more or less how much further I would fall if I did fall? Good question. I let out a nervous laugh.

When she heard that answer, Aileen's eyes got wide. She immediately sprang into action. She covered the last distance to where I was in a split second.

I carefully looked down and could see my foot had caught a branch growing out of the hillside. It was not a big branch, just the start of a small tree. But it had given me something to slow down my slide. It would not hold me long, or provide any way up from where I was. But, it was likely what kept me from sliding all the way down - more so than my desperate scrambling.

Standing over me now, Aileen could see the situation and that the branch was not going to do much for me for long. She knelt down and braced herself on a small rock nearby. She grabbed my arm and said, "I got you." Pulling up on my arm, she was giving me an edge - an opening to climb up. I tried pushing against the cliffside with my feet, but it wasn't doing much good.

Aileen kept pulling. It was amazing. Aileen must have dragged me six inches higher above the tiny limb. I weighed more than she did, but that didn't slow her down. In the background, I heard Kelly making some sort of joke about us rushing ahead. Aileen kept a firm hold on me and kept pulling. As she pulled me up, I could maneuver my leg. My arms still had nothing to grab on to, but I started to swing my leg up. With Aileen's help, I was able to get one knee above the cliffside. My other leg was still over the edge, but I was stable. With that knee and my hands on firm ground, I pulled myself all the way up. Aileen didn't let go the whole time. Once I was up, she sat back against the part of the path that stepped up at that point. She pulled me in closer, away from the edge.

I was so relieved. So grateful. Felt a bit of triumph, but was shaking like mad. Aileen was exhausted, but also relieved. She was dusty and tousled, but had a big smile on her face. Her face looked weary at the same time. I wanted to kiss her. I don't remember if I did. I do remember that her actions were not that of an average civilian. Aileen was trained the way I had been - she was calm in the face of danger. She had skills to rely on, skills to save my life. She must be with the Agency, too?!

At that moment, Kelly came bounding along. Still kind of joking.

"Look at you two," she said. "All dusty and a mess. What have you been up to?"

"Anthony really did fall, Kelly. I just pulled him up." Aileen was scanning the hillside across the ravine from where we sat. She was looking for something.

"What? Crazy. Wow - I thought you guys were joking around," Kelly said as she took in the dirt and scrapes on both of us. She could see the trail of drag marks from the cliffside to where we sat.

I looked at Aileen again. "Sweetie, what about your knee?"

Aileen looked down. Her knee was bleeding, dripping down her leg. "Wow. I must've scraped it up on that rock over there. I hadn't noticed."

The rock that gave her leverage also ripped into her knee while she was pulling me up. I was dusty and shaken up, but had no real scrapes or bruises. Aileen was the one who had the physical reminder of the crazy near fall, and the effort to get me back up.

We took a moment to collect ourselves. Then, when we stood up, we checked out the rest of this 'path' I'd found. It quickly disappeared to the left, leaving no sign of how it would safely lead down to the water below. So, we laughed it off and took one more look over the side where I'd almost fallen. It was quite a ways down - 20 or 30 feet at the least. That little branch was the only thing before a long, steep dropoff down below. I may not have died on the fall. I certainly could have, but I definitely would've broken many limbs, and would've been in a remote spot hard to rescue. Wow, that was a close call.

My heart sang on the final stretch of the way down to the water. I'm sure I was smiling ear-to-ear. Luckily, the shock of the near death experience was enough to explain my giddiness to Kelly. I'm not sure if Aileen picked up on the energy I had. Yes, she could see I was giddy. But, did she know it was more about her role as an Agent than it was about her saving my life. I knew what near death experiences were like as an Agent. I was always experiencing that danger, that exhilaration afterwards once I had survived. The fiero experience like winning a video game challenge, but ten fold, because it was real life, real danger. I'm sure I was letting a bit of that show through too.

But, the real energy in my step, the real source of my beaming expressions and hearty laughs was the waves of realizations hitting me about me and Aileen. I could finally open up and be myself. Let her know why I was there in Monterey. Truly, why I was there. Hell, she probably already knew. They had sent her there to protect me. To work with me.

But, she had been there months before me. How could they know I'd be there and in danger? I am clearly in danger. The near accident on the motorcycle had a new meaning for me now. Krieg had saved my life for sure, but in more ways than he realized. If someone was trying to kill me, why didn't he just shoot me? Why the car accident? That analysis could come later. I also started asking myself questions about the accident in Arvada. Was that connected too?

But then, back in the present, what about Aileen? Of course, she wasn't there specifically for me, but for whomever was going to come to fill out the team and finish the project. It could have been Sven, Hancock, any of the others. But, it wasn't - it was me.

Was she the project lead or was I? Damn, maybe I'm just here to support her. And today the boss had to bail me out? So confusing.

So, then, was our chemistry real? Or had she put on a show, to draw me in closer? Oh, the doubts were seeping in. If only Kelly weren't there, I could talk to Aileen. Soon enough, we'd be alone, where we could talk. But, was it soon enough?

I had to know. This could turn my life upside down. In a good way! Meeting her and falling in love - that had turned my life upside down. This could put it all right side up again. I had been wrestling with making a tough choice. Now, a third path was opening up. God, I needed to talk to her, and soon.

We made our way back to the main road, looking for that path down. It was only another five minutes along the road before we saw the real path down to the water. It jumped out at us clear as day. The near-death experience of almost falling down that cliff side was totally avoidable. We made our way to a group of large rocks that provided easy access to the river. It looked inviting and cool. A good way to relax after the stress of the hike down.

None of us had our swimsuits on. We needed to change. I found a spot behind some rocks, wrapped my towel around my waist and did the old swap under the towel trick. I tied off my trunks, then went to put my shorts away in our bag. I looked closely at my underwear and ran off to tell the ladies.

"Seems like I split the seam right down the backside of my boxers! Can you believe it?"

They both laughed a good one at that.

Somewhere in the physical stress of falling, catching myself, or being pulled up by Aileen, I had ripped my underwear. Crazy!

After we had been swimming awhile, Aileen looked at me and just said, "Jeez! That was crazy." I knew exactly what she was saying.

Awhile later I said to her, "Can you believe that? Thank you!"

Finally, after enjoying the water and the beautiful surroundings, it was time to get back. Our misadventure on the way down had slowed us down. It cut off our time at the river a bit. Walking back seemed really quick. It was incredibly clear how to find the path up and the road back. As we passed the area where we tried to walk down and I had slipped, it seemed crazy that we had even tried. There was no real path there. Maybe mountain goats or chipmunks or some other woodland creature could use it to get around. But, no people had ever gone there, before us at least. Dumb!

We got back in the Half Car and headed back to Monterey. Of course, the ride back was along those narrow, treacherous, and dramatic miles up the coast. It was always full of great views. But, my nerves were shot and I could hardly look at the dropoffs and cliffs along the way. It was not enjoyable scenery that afternoon. Then my training kicked in. I had to be aware of what was happening - I may not be in control while Kelly drives, but with awareness and planning, I could jump in as needed.

Kelly seemed unbothered by the events of the day. She hurried back toward Monterey at speeds higher than most locals would dare drive on that road on a normal day. She cranked her head to the backseat to look Aileen in the eye as they were talking. I had the close-up view from the front seat - seeing every curve and cliff, watching each move to make sure we were in safe territory along the way. If our margins got out of truly acceptable range, I'd be ready to reach over and steady the wheel.

Kelly had her bag of chips up front, propped between the seats, just behind the stick shift. She'd hold the wheel with one hand, shift gears, then pop her other hand into the bag, hunting for crumbs. As she found some good munchies, she'd be deep in a story for Aileen, turning back to make this or that point. A few times, my instincts wondered if I was going to die in that Half Car. Escape the danger on the cliff leading to Arroyo Seco, then die at the hands of Kelly's loose and fast driving. But, my trained eye kept a calm watch, always knowing when Kelly needed to return her attention back to the road and the curves. She always did, she always did.

In the end, we made it to Carmel where the road comes back inland and the risk of plummeting to one's death goes away. What a day of adventure!

Chapter Sixteen

AFTER THE SWIM

That was it. Three tries and three failures. Time to move along.

He had hit the dirt beneath Rogue at just the right timing. He could see it all come together so nicely. No motorbike driver to pull him through the mess. Just a hiking accident to snuff him out.

But, then she came along. Damn, who was she? Sure, he knew Rogue had hiking companions. But, who was the one who pulled him up?

With reflexes and skills like that, she had to be an Agent. Doug Krieg on the motorbike had simply been a lucky stroke for Rogue - unusually prepared for such a car accident. But, not an Agent. Schelletz did his homework afterwards and confirmed Krieg was not in the game.

Today, though, was no special case. She used skills he'd seen before. She was even scanning the hillside as she helped up Rogue. She knew something was up and was not going to let things get out of control anymore that afternoon. Schelletz was ready to shoot out that branch, leaving Rogue to fall to his death after his lucky foot scramble. But that was out of the question. The Oligarchs wanted this to look like an accident. She'd see the gun shot from his hillside placement. The Agency would know someone had assassinated Rogue. Schelletz could not allow that. Damn the Oligarchs' strict orders on that front. He still could not see why.

But wait, maybe they would be lenient with him. Sure, he'd failed three times, but making an 'accident' happen was much different than a point blank hit. They knew that, right?

Ah, but he'd promised he could do it as an accident. Assured them of his masterful skills. They had put up half the payoff out front to make sure he'd stay focused on their job until it was done. And quite a sum it was.

There was no time to waste. He left the gun there, didn't pack it up, didn't bring it with him. Sure, it had value. But, it's value was useless if he was dead. Someone might find it one day, but he was careful on every job to be 100% certain no evidence would point anyone back at him. So, no need to hide the evidence. He sped off as fast as he could, getting back to the motorbike he'd used to get up into the hills.

Along the way, his phone rang. He knew it would be the Oligarchs. He threw the phone down into the river below. Three strikes and you are out. There was nothing he could tell them to explain the outcome. They didn't want to hear it. He didn't want to waste time explaining how his plan had failed. The only thing he could accomplish by answering would be to give them some data to help them track him down.

Schelletz was already three steps into disappearing into the woodwork. He had a flight to Hong Kong, making his way to Berlin a few days and a few more flights later. "Schelletz" would disappear from the world. 3 months later or so, a Scottish migrant named "Claidheamh" would appear, ready for assignments. Not for the Oligarchs - never getting that close. But, ready to be of service for sure. If Schelletz could pull off each step, he could avoid the deadly fate the Oligarchs had in mind for him - and get back into this game that felt so natural to him.

A few months of quiet time would be nice, in fact. Quite nice.

Chapter Seventeen

TALKING

Kelly dropped us off in front of Aileen's place.

"Thanks, Kelly." Aileen said right away.

"Yeah, thanks. I'll get out here." I was being the gentleman to walk her in. "I'll make my own way home."

Kelly took off in her Half Car, and we were alone.

"We have got to talk!" I was about to burst.

"But not here. Let's go to the lab." She headed toward the lab building.

As I followed, there was a distance there. We didn't speak, we didn't touch. Just two people with an urgency in their step.

My mind raced in 8 different directions. The choice I made on Valentine's Day - it had been so hard. This was new information, making the whole thought process somewhat irrelevant.

Who's the boss? Am I leading the project, or is she? Why has she been in Monterey all this time? Are there aspects of the project

I am not aware of? How does this impact our relationship? Is our relationship genuine, or had I been played? That last one lingered.

I caught up to her. I could sense an easing in her stance, in her step. As I narrowed the physical distance, the emotional distance was relieved as well. Instinctively, I reached out and grabbed her hand. I started to think better of it, but her warmth was reassuring and she gently squeezed my hand. Still no words, but we were connecting.

We got to the lab and did a quick sweep to make sure no one was around, then we headed into my small office.

We stood for a moment and looked at each other. There was urgency to get here, lots to discuss, but in that moment, what we needed was to take each other in slowly and carefully. I looked at her face, into her eyes, carefully.

"Ok, so I suppose I have some explaining to do." She smiled warmly.

"Yes. Clearly, you are with the Agency. I saw in the way you responded at Arroyo Seco. You saved my life. Have I said thank you yet, for saving my life?" I was gentle, calm, sincere, with a bit of a smile on my face.

"Yes, you have said thank you. And you are right I am with the Agency. Have been for 7 years. I've been involved with a number of different missions and longer term projects. This one is the highlight so far." Aileen let out a sigh of relief, sharing this information.

"What about the project? What does this do to the project?" I went back into feeling confused.

"Nothing. Only a few people know who I am. That should not interfere with me directing the project as I have all along." Aileen slowed down as she said the last few words.

"I thought so. I am your wingman, eh? And here I thought I was running the show," I said with a jovial tone.

Aileen pondered for a moment, then she started in, "It made sense to let you believe you were running it. I mean you were running it, but not alone. It helped a ton that we had a relationship, and I could, uh…, influence your thinking on some things."

"I never told you about the kids and their real situation, where I had to make choices and decisions." I was a bit bewildered, maybe even defensive at this point.

Aileen calmed my frayed ego. "But, as someone in on the project, updated on every aspect of it, I knew what was going on. I knew what deeper questions you were wrestling with. So, I could give advice that resonated on two levels."

"That's my next question. I'm afraid to ask it... Was our relationship just a ploy to be close to me? Or is there something real there?" I asked this plainly, looking for information, not emotion.

"Anthony, come here. Look in my eyes. Look at me."

She paused as I slowly came around, looked in her eyes, grabbed her hands in mine.

"Does this seem fake? What do you feel right now? Listen to your heart."

I looked at her. I started to tear up. "It feels real," I said almost inaudibly. I was really putting myself out there. I had done that on Valentine's Day, but this was a new level of exposure.

"Yes, Anthony, it is real. We don't choose these things. They just happen."

"I want to kiss you." The last time I said those words, it was a simple expression of desire. This time, it was more of a request for permission. To my boss?!

Just like the last time, Aileen leaned in, grabbed my shirt and pulled me closer. We kissed, and it felt as right as it always had. Nothing had changed. Nothing ... had ... changed. Nothing had changed!

"Aileen, this is so great. You know why?"

"I think I can guess. It feels great to me too." She smiled.

But she didn't get it. How could she know.

"You were worried about the You Only Live Twice rule."

"What?! Did someone tell you? Someone in the Agency."

"No ... Wait, were you talking to someone in the Agency about me?" She looked concerned.

"Yeah, I had too. I was so conflicted. I talked to Hal."

"Ah, ok. That's no big deal. I trust Hal." Aileen sighed with relief.

"So, yeah, the You Only Live Twice rule. I care so much about you that I couldn't keep seeing you and stay in the Agency. I couldn't risk that. I either needed to let you go, or let the Agency go."

"But, you are still seeing me? I don't understand." Aileen looked puzzled.

"Once this project was complete in a few months, I was going to take action. I made up my mind before Valentine's Day." I was clear with resolve.

"And..."

"And now I don't have to choose. We are both in the Agency. You can look out for yourself. We can look after each other, as you demonstrated today. It's the absolutely best outcome ever." I was smiling ear to ear.

"Now hold on a minute, Mr. Rogue. You are not off the hook here. What were you going to do? What decision had you made."

I got down on one knee, looking down on the ground. My eyes slowly traveled from her feet, up her legs and waistline. As my eyes reached her arm, I put out my hands to hold her hand between my two hands. My eyes traveled up her neck, past her lips and to her eyes. She was smiling and starting to tear up at this point.

"I choose you. I have always chosen you. Ms. Stirling, will you marry me?"

I always thought I would be shaking when I asked a woman to marry me. The ultimate act of putting yourself out there. Telling someone that you want to spend your life together. Not knowing for sure what the answer will be. Hoping that the person you were opening up to would want precisely the same thing.

But, in this moment, I was steady as a rock. Absolutely confident. Not confident in her response - how can you be confident until you ask. But, confident that this was right. That I needed to tell Aileen that I wanted to spend my life with her, regardless of the outcome.

"Yes." She smiled and said it firmly and clearly.

I stood up and embraced her, wrapped my arms around her. We were both so happy.

Chapter Eighteen

WMD

With the 1000 Words system and Evan's training, the project was coming to its active phase. No more training, no more prep work. These kids were ready for prime time.

"Anthony, did you hear the news reports this morning?" Lev asked.

"What do you mean?"

"There has been an attack in Syria. Early reports make it sound like the regime used chemical weapons on their own people."

"What? That is crazy." I was shocked by this sad news.

"Yeah. It was a rebel stronghold. They had been using conventional forces to drive the rebels out of a neighborhood outside of Damascus."

"The capital? This went down in the capital?" My shock and horror escalated.

"The rebels were holding strong. So, this morning, Damascus time, a few rockets came falling in this rebel neighborhood. Folks ran for cover as they've done in other attacks. They thought they'd be ok inside. Or that once the rockets had made impact and their house was still standing, that they were ok. But, then, a white cloud drifted across the neighborhood, coming from the rockets."

"My god, chemicals?!"

"They collapsed on the ground, choking. Hundreds of people - men, women and children - asphyxiated. No chance to get away. Chemical weapons indeed. This is the most active use of WMD since Saddam Hussein gassed the Kurdish people in Iraq in the 1990s." Lev was clearly outraged by the story he was sharing.

"How can they be sure? Do they know it was the regime who launched this?"

"That's where we come in. The kids are going to do their magic. We need some hard data, one way or the other by tomorrow." Lev was revved up.

"Wow. This is a big one, Lev."

"They are ready for it. Here's the thing. Evan gave me a suggestion during their final training last week. Actually, it was more than a suggestion. It's a definitive rule about running analysis with these tools. We need the kids to work independently."

"Really? They often work together so well. Why would we want to split them up in the analysis?" I was confused by Evan's new rule.

"Statistically, if we have one conclusion come out of the process, it has a 15% likelihood of being accurate and actionable. But, the more analysts finding the same or similar conclusion, the higher the likely accuracy. With Evan's tools, the Center for Nonproliferation Studies' data, and the analysis of these kids, if all three reach the same conclusion, it's 92% likely to be accurate."

"Wow. 92%? That's amazing. In all the work I've done with the Agency, we are rarely that confident about an analysis." This made me proud to be on this project.

"Yeah, well the Iraq war taught us all lessons about how policy makers can get overly confident with the information we provide. We need to be absolutely transparent when we draw conclusions, so they can recommend an action that fits the situation."

"We can never be 100%, Lev. But, 92% accuracy! that is powerful."

"Ok, let's get your kids in here and get crunching." Lev's eagerness continued.

The kids were finishing their morning training at the DLI when the word reached them. They got cleaned up and headed to the lab early so I could brief them. I had closed the academic lab for the college for the day.

"Good morning, guys. Today is a big day, we have a hot one."

"Really? What's up, Anthony?" Earl said.

"We need to track the origin of some WMD. Some chemicals."

"Is this about the attack in Syria?" Alice chimed in.

"You got it, Alice. We are being asked to analyze the source of the attack. Where did it come from? Was it really a chemical attack? Who ordered it? So, put aside the speculation you saw in the news, and let's look for hard data in our database.

"Ah, ok. How long do we have?" Alice asked.

"They need something tomorrow morning, our best analysis at the time."

"Short, but doable. With the three of us working together, we've solved some simulations in less time."

"Here's the thing. I've set you up with three separate analysis systems. We need you each to work independently. Mr. Leavy told Lev that we can be more certain of an analysis if we can get two or three of you to come to similar conclusions through independent investigations."

"But, Anthony..." Earl trailed off.

"We can do this!" Alice shot him a glance.

"I have great confidence in you. So does Lev. You are all top notch analysts with these tools. You have worked hard and taken on all the skills we set out for you. Now let's put them to work and see what you come up with."

Lev came into the meeting room. "I just got off the phone with the DLI. Their listening posts around Syria have been on high alert since the event happened. I've gotten access to the transcripts of their sessions from the past 6 months, up to about an hour ago. It's all been merged into the Nonproliferation database. We'll update a few times during the day to get you all the latest and greatest."

The three analysts got setup on their different 1000 Words systems. It was a bit slow going and tentative at first. I could see them looking around, like they wanted to check in with each other about approach or findings.

I talked with Lev about it. "We built their skills as a team. They are used to the dynamic of discussion, constructing knowledge together, bouncing ideas off each other."

"I know. I am concerned about that too. But, I am confident in these kids. They are all bright. You didn't select them in Monument Valley based on their teamwork. You found them independently. And, we need that triangulation process to support any conclusions we draw for the Agency."

"I've been checking in. Alice is trying lots of things, making some progress. Earl seems deep into a thread, but I think he'd feel better to have some support knowing that others see it as a fruitful approach. And Jason is moving slow. He has been generating creative theories, but is a bit stumped as to how to test them, where to dig to start finding connections and relevant data. I'm just nervous. I can't see any of them getting to a fruitful theory anytime soon."

"Slow down, Anthony. Give them some space and some time. Do you feel like they are well-trained?" Lev exuded confidence.

"Well, yeah. You and I built the plan together and got them these great experiences over the past year. They are well trained. I mean no one has ever been trained to do what they are specialists at. So, who knows if it is effective. But, our exercises and simulations thus far have proven interesting and successful. Don't you think?"

"Absolutely! That's why I'm not worrying about this task - this question. It is one more exercise for them. They will produce some sort of useful outcome. I don't know what it will be. None of us do, or we wouldn't need their analysis, right? But, whatever it is, they will have become better at this analytical process. You and I will know the process better. So, they can improve, and we can identify any additional training needed."

"But, Lev, I..."

"Stop!" Lev cut me off. "Trust, Anthony. Just take a few deep breaths. Go back to the kids. See what support they need. But, trust and let them do their work."

I took a few deep breaths. I looked at Lev for a moment. He looked up, smiled, and waved me away with a quick flick of his wrist. So, I walked my way back to the stations for the analysts.

We paused for some lunch. The analysts stayed in separate areas, but all took a break in waves for a bite. I was able to sit with each of them. I asked how it was going, then just listened. I didn't want to distort their process.

"I'm tracking down snippets here and there," explained Alice. "There was no huge cache of documents or transcripts that gave an aha moment. But, I am making my way through a large subset of the data, finding a few specific pieces that support the idea the government carried out the attack."

She was finding mostly circumstantial evidence. Nothing that could make a good case in court. But, you could wrap a compelling story around it. My sense was if she continued to have small successes to add to her evidence, she'd reach a critical mass, and then the dominoes would all fall and the picture would be made plain. But, how long would that take, and would she hit a cold, dead end at some point.

Next, I visited with Jason. "Well, I have 8 subsets of data I've been collecting. I am not finding a lot of connections between them. The trail seems to fall dead between these clusters. Each cluster makes sense - like one has to do with the known weapons program in Syria, another has to do with the neighborhood where the attack happened, another is communications between military outposts in the last few days, and so on. I'm working really hard to connect them. But when I use 1000 Words to smash the various clusters together, no links emerge. So, I've resorted to browsing through some of the documents in the clusters to see if there is a new way to reorganize them, or some themes I can manually search on. It's getting kind of tedious."

I could see Jason was engaged in the puzzle. He had spent some time coming up with an approach that could work. Now, after investing his time in that process and picking the approach he thought had the most likely chance of success, he was set on this path. He was determined to play it out until he found a lead, not able to imagine another or a better approach.

Earl was a bit strung out when he paused for lunch. I think he was really hungry. It seemed like he had such a focused burst of activity in the morning that he didn't want to interrupt it with lunch. But, now he was crashing a bit due to hunger.

"Wow! This sandwich is good. But, I'd eat sandpaper if you gave it to me for lunch right now. I am so hungry." Earl was talkative.

"I'm glad you like the sandwiches. I'd like to say I made them myself. But, I can say I ordered them up at the bakery with each of you in mind. I figured you were a melty cheese kind of guy. So, how is the research coming?"

"Anthony, let me say this. I have tried every approach I can think of. They all are leading to dead ends. I started with rebels who lived in the area to see what government communications had to say about them. What did the authorities know about their whereabouts? Would they know to attack this neighborhood? What did the regime have to gain? Then, I went after information focused on the President and his battle against the democratic uprising. Did he signal his willingness to use these weapons? Were there signs he had reached this level of frustration with his regime unraveling? Then, I tried to take a geographic approach for awhile - movements of government troops that indicate an offensive being planned. Or perhaps they moved their troops specifically out of harms way?"

"Do you need more to eat?" I asked.

"Yes, that would be great. I wasn't going to ask, but this will be a long day. So, I went searching for data on all of these theories and rapidly hit dead ends. Each time I'd back up and try a new approach. I think I'm on my 13th approach to this puzzle. None has led to solid evidence. I'm not sure at this point whether to keep generating the approaches until one sticks better. Or to pick up one that had been an immediate failure and see if it has any depth or other element hiding that we missed."

I talked with Earl without really answering his question at this point, if I interjected with ideas or advice, it might well reflect the paths Alice or Jason were taking. That would mess with our independent confirmation we were aiming for, so I held back. The analysts were making progress, each in his or her own way. I could relax a bit more knowing the movement that was happening. They all had the potential to get somewhere meaningful at least. But, would they actually get there? Was the data there to support any or all of their approaches? Time would tell.

After lunch, Earl started hitting pay dirt.

"I think I have something," Earl came to me in the evening.

"Let me look this over," I replied.

He actually went back and looked at what he could find from all of his lucky 13 approaches so far. When he laid out his most salient conclusions, he could see how they would piece together for a compelling case. It looked a bit like Alice's circumstantial case, but with more meat on its bones. Instead of starting with the conclusion the government did it, Earl had just asked discrete questions. The answers to those questions lined up in a way to make the compelling case that it was the actions of the regime. As he pulled at a few more strands of data here and there, his case became more solid. He was finding evidence Alice had not stumbled on, troop movements and orders from military advisers.

"Earl, this does look like a solid conclusion. Keep working it the way you started, asking specific, open questions and following what the data tells you. Don't base them on the theory the regime did it, just keep them open. As you have this right now, we could present it with moderate confidence to the Agency. But, let's see what more you can build out to make the case that much clearer."

"Ok, got it, Anthony." Earl dove back in.

Lev came to me with news that they'd added some additional DLI data mid day.

"Shouldn't we have let the analysts know?"

"With this first burst, I wanted to see if they picked up on the change themselves. We've got another update coming in about an hour. Did any of the analysts note the change?"

"No, I haven't heard anything from any of them about additional data. Earl has a good analysis developing. He's back in doing more work to flesh it out. But, he didn't mention the data."

"Ok, keep me posted. I'll let you know when the second dump of DLI data comes."

A half hour later Alice came to find me. "Anthony, I think I have something. Can I talk through it with you?"

"Absolutely, let's go look at your 1000 Words."

Alice began, "So, I kept digging into various files from that subset I told you about. Boy, was that a slog! You know, a few hours ago, a big chunk of new data appeared that I hadn't seen. I opened a few and they were transcripts of phone and radio communication from earlier today."

"Lev just told me they dumped a load of new DLI intercepts into the database midday."

"Yeah, that makes sense. Those were them. Well, they turned out to be a gold mine. Makes sense that the fresh data would prove useful. So, there were some military communications in there. Some commanders near the attack freaking out. I guess a few of their men were impacted by the chemicals." Alice showed concern on her face.

"So, do you think the regime wasn't behind it? If their troops were caught off guard."

"Oh no, my data is pointing pretty clearly at the regime. Well, it is subtle, but repeated over and over again. In those communications between platoons and leadership, the commanders are very calm about the attack, leaving clear indications they knew what was coming."

"Can you give me an example?" I asked Alice for more.

"Sure, here is a report from this morning our time, mid-day in Syria. There is a commander from a station about 10 miles southwest of the site of the attack. He called the regional command post to report a faint white cloud that drifted toward his field site, from the north east. One of his men walked into the white cloud and came out hacking, with burning eyes. The medic on staff pulled him aside and he stabilized him. When the commander made the call, his man still had a bit of a burn in his throat and a splitting headache, especially behind his eyes. The regional command listened intently. In part of his response, the regional command officer starts to talk about how the radius should have only been 3 miles. When the field commander asks what radius he is talking about, the discussion is halted abruptly."

"So, like you said, some sense a regional commander knew what was happening. But, no smoking gun."

"Yeah, but this has allowed me to dig deeper on the regional command post and it's staff. With the documents I found this morning, then this conversation where regional command let's a few things slip, I was able to turn up a trail of communications dating back 6 weeks. Each one on their own is vague and noncommittal. But, now that I can tie them together, it's an undeniable direct chain that shows an order being produced and followed." Alice showed confidence.

"How far up does it go? All the way to the Syrian President?"

"I can't make that claim, but it does get into centralized military command."

"Wow, ok. Great work! Keep at it. See if you can get a bead on what the Syrian President knew and when he knew it"

"Got it!" Alice was excited.

Lev let me know the second DLI update had been added and that I could share that with the analysts. I popped in quickly on Alice and Earl to let them know, and they continued with their research.

From there, I checked in on Jason. He had not come out lately and I was getting worried about his progress.

"Anthony, I need someone to talk to, to free up my mind a bit. I'm glad you are here."

"Always happy, Jason." I was supportive.

"I have tried every angle I can think of to fulfill my original analysis. We are 10 hours into this, and my trail has gone cold. If my original analysis is off, I have to start all over - I'm back to square one."

"I can hear your frustration, Jason. Here's the thing. We just updated the database with new DLI listening post transcripts. This is fresh data from today, from communication intercepted in the last 12-24 hours. So you can refresh your analysis, run through it again and see where these new data points lead you."

"Fresh data?! Do you know that it will help me? What do you know about what is in there?" Jason was confused.

"Ha. Nothing. I know nothing about their content. That's what we have you and your amigos for. Go back in there, dig around, and see what this new data does for you!"

"Ok. Cool. I'm excited. I can retrace my steps in a tenth of the time it took me to get here. Give me an hour and I'll know more. Ok!"

He almost ran back into his analysis room, he was so excited.

I stepped out for a decaf mocha. This had been a stressful day and I needed an indulgence to keep up my enthusiasm. I could smell the sea air, hear the sea lions barking, feel the mist on my face. This was a beautiful place. I was lucky to spend a year there, lucky to find my love there.

But, I needed to get back to our work. I made my way back to the lab. Lev was chatting with Alice and Earl at the main lab table.

"Come sit with us, Anthony!"

"But, Lev, why are they chatting?"

"They are both done, Anthony. They completed their analyses while you were out walking. The docs are being reviewed, but they are ready to handoff to the Agency so the president can be briefed in the morning."

"Wow, ok. How did it go?"

Alice chimed in, "Well, we came to the same conclusion. Talking just now, we got there in very different ways. But a good number of our key documents overlapped. We have compelling evidence the regime did this. They knew about it ahead of time and had planned for it. This was no accident, and the Ministry of Defense was involved."

"Wow, Alice, you sound confident." I challenged her a bit.

"I know this data now, Anthony. It's hard to walk away with any other conclusion."

"That's great to hear. Now, once Jason shares his analysis, we'll be in business."

"What was that? Did I hear my name?" Jason's voice came from around the corner.

Lev boomed from the table, "Jason, my boy. Do you have a case to make?" Jason nodded. "Then show us what you have."

"Is it ok?" Jason didn't want to reveal too much in front of the other analysts.

"They have already submitted their work. At this point, there is no cross-pollinating possible." Lev assured him.

"Ah, ok." Jason looked a little stressed, feeling the pressure to confirm their findings.

I reassured him, "Look, buddy, it is what it is. Everyone's work is done. Have confidence in how you broke this down. Tell us a story."

Jason took a deep breath, then pulled up his data set in 1000 Words and started in. He walked through his 8 clusters that he had told me about. With a few quick combinations, he was able to remove a ton of extraneous data points. Then he crossed the communications of the military posts with the news media out of the town under attack. With the latest transcribed data handed off about an hour ago, he was able to make some strong connections. He uncovered a number of discussions with the regional commander that all pointed to the regime having carried out the attack. Because of his 8 pile approach, though, he got deeper into the network than the others got to. He was able to trace the regional commander from Alice's example call to a meeting at the ministry of defense about a month prior. At that meeting, the minister made it clear that the President had authorized the use of chemical weapons to bring the population in line.

His conclusion came together well. His analysis walked paths not explored by the other analysts. But a number of sign posts ended up guiding all of them to similar findings. We had our 3 for 3, to get our confidence level into the 90s.

The Navajo kids, they were still kids, laughed and joked and traded notes. They were appropriately excited about the overlap that had occurred in their analysis. Already, their reports were getting packaged up for the Agency's DC team to pickup in the morning to update the President.

Later that night, I briefed Aileen, the boss, about our progress, and the success the kids had in their efforts with the data sets. The next day, the President appeared at a press conference to discuss the events in Syria. Aileen and I sat together to listen to the discussion of Syria.

"Good morning. Good morning. Thank you all for coming. I need to talk with you all about the tragedy that has befallen the Syrian people. In the bloody civil war raging there, we turned an awful corner yesterday. I'm sure you all have seen the videos of victims laying lifeless, horrific in the story they tell. Civilians trying to piece their lives back together. Well, I can tell you this morning, with strong confidence - this was the act of the Syrian regime. Desperate, isolated more and more by the community of nations, they crossed a line today. A line put in place 70 years ago and agreed to by all nations at that time. No one wanted to see the horrors of chemical warfare that befell so many in World War I. But, the Syrian government showed themselves this week willing to work outside of international norms. This behavior cannot be tolerated. Which is why I am bringing plans to diminish that nation's capacity for using weapons of mass destruction to the US Congress. We need to come together and stand up for what is right for the people of Syria, and for stability around the globe."

Chapter Nineteen

DRIVING TO THE AIRPORT

The Navajo team was getting situated, settling into their roles, and being called on for analysis and support. It had been a long year, finding the right candidates, putting together the experts in Monterey, giving the kids the right mix of experience and challenge. But, now they were gelling as a team, adding a new capability that the Agency had never had before.

Aileen and I had told our families about the engagement and we were making plans for our wedding. She came from Minnesota, so we wanted to have an outdoor, summer wedding there. It was scheduled for the following summer, to give time to book the garden and the other arrangements. We were both excited about this new phase of our lives. In the meantime, the Agency was looking for new assignments for us both, a way that we could team up.

At MIIS, we had both made good friends with a professor named Kurt Johns. He was from Britain originally, but had settled in California 20 years earlier. Kurt was headed to England with his wife and two boys for the summer to reconnect with family and colleagues on that side of the the Pond. He had asked Aileen and I to house sit. We jumped at the chance to play house together - care for the animals, water the plants, tend the garden. We both liked Kurt and his family and were happy to help.

The day of their departure, we all were driving to the airport in San Francisco, so that Aileen and I could use their Volvo wagon to take care of the affairs of the house while they were gone. Kurt was behind the wheel, his wife Diane and their 10 year old James were sharing the passenger front seat. In the back sat Alex, their 12 year old, me in the middle, then Aileen.

As we made our way up the 101 from Salinas through Gilroy and the other coastal towns, Kurt had kept moderate speed. About 20 minutes into the ride, Diane looked back and realized Alex wasn't wearing his belt. In fact, Kurt was the only person wearing one - the rest of us had neglected to pull them on, as we were jockeying around to figure out how we would all fit. So, with that gentle reminder from Diane, we all grabbed our belts and buckled up.

As we made our way through San Jose, we connected with the faster expressways of the larger San Francisco area.

"I used to take the 101 all the way to the airport, but I learned about an alternate route two years ago," Kurt said. "I'll jump on 280 where the traffic is lighter, we can cut over near the airport, and it will shave 15 minutes off our drive."

Kurt found the expressways more comfortable and picked up his speed - I looked over his shoulder and saw him hovering between 75 and 80.

The route along 280 was actually quite pretty. It led into and through the hills along the peninsula, passing towns like Los Altos Hills and Portola Valley, but with a lot of open space. It even led along the edge of a large fish and game reserve which includes a reservoir and some county parks. It was typical California countryside, browned out grass along hillsides, trees spotted here and there, with some larger partial forests higher in the hills. Compared to the over-built Silicon Valley 101 scenery, this was relaxing and gorgeous. Aileen and I talked about the landscape as we passed by, and I reached out for her hand at one point.

"What kind of plans do you have for your time in the UK?" I asked Kurt and his family.

"It's England. We're going to visit England, son." Kurt smiled back at me. "My dad is getting older and has been ill..."

"So we want to have a good chunk of time to visit him," Diane chimed in.

"We'll hike in the countryside, visit some National Trust sites near my parents," Kurt continued.

"Do you boys have anything special you want to do?" Aileen asked.

Before Alex or James could respond, we heard a loud bang and the car shook.

"What the heck was that?" I asked?

"Hold on! I think we lost a tire," Kurt said as he looked around and started to make his way to the far right lane and the shoulder, across 4 lanes of California expressway. I grabbed Aileen's hand tighter. We were totally in Kurt's hands, with no way to call upon any of our emergency training.

There was an exit up ahead and he was clearly headed there. As he moved the car to the right, he used the brakes to slow down and the Volvo began to fish tail.

"You're fish tailing," I said. Kurt was making his way toward that exit, but clearly not fully in control.

As we got to the side of the road, we went too far, onto the shoulder, then off the road and started part ways up a hill. The car had slowed, but was still going 65.

Once we left the road and hit the bank, the car rolled onto it's side, the driver's side, and starting sliding back across the roadway. Where the car was and exactly what was happening was unclear. All we knew was that none of us was in control anymore.

No one was making a sound, but as I sat there, hung there suspended by that seatbelt with the car sliding uncontrollably, I had one thought. "Here comes the impact!" I braced for what I assumed would be the inevitable thud of a car going highway speeds slamming into the roof of our car as it pointed south along the expressway. I assumed that would be the next step in this horrible journey. I figured our chances of surviving that were slim. I waited - one, two, three, four, five seconds. No impact. We kept sliding for what seemed like minutes. I'm sure it was mere seconds.

I heard a crunch and felt a solid bump, but this was not the impact I had expected. The car was tilting again, this time back to the right, to the passenger side. We hit level, then titled a bit up on the right side - I slid into Aileen. Finally, we tilted back left and landed on the wheels as the car came to rest.

I took a deep breath, squeezed Aileen's hand and looked over at her. She seemed ok.

"Is everyone ok?" Aileen spoke up first.

Still looking at her, "I'm good I said."

Diane was turned and looking behind her, to see where the car was. "We are on the median, not in a lane... uh…, I'm ok, maybe bruised. Boys?"

"I think I am ok. The seatbelt dug into my side a bit, but I am ok." said James.

Alex opened his door, leaned out and vomited, then said, "Uhh, wow. I'm better now that I did that. I think I was just dizzy."

"I'm good," Kurt said abruptly as he popped out his door and came back to look in on Alex.

"And you, Aileen?" I said.

"Yep, good, fine," she said, smiling back at me.

As Kurt opened the door to check on Alex, stepping around the vomit, a man came sprinting across the roadway from the right shoulder.

"Are y'all ok? If you're ok, step on outta there." The man said from outside the car.

He led everyone out the driver side, where there was no traffic going by. I took a look at this guy - he was wearing overalls from a car repair shop. His nameplate on the overalls said "Lucky."

Lucky looked us over as he gave a direct report of what happened. "I saw the whole thing from behind you. As soon as I saw the fish tailing, I pulled over to be ready to help once you came to a stop. I can't believe you all slid across all that traffic and no one hit you. Y'all are lucky!"

"No, you are Lucky," I said pointing at his nameplate. He laughed heartily - that can't be the first time he had heard that. The kids giggled too - not sure if they were laughing at my joke, or just enjoying Lucky's hearty laugh. After that, the mood loosened up a bit.

"Boys, make sure you stay close to the guardrail and away from traffic," Kurt said.

"I can't believe we are standing on the median in the middle of 280 with traffic whizzing by," Diane said as she looked around us. We all looked around in wonder as well. I saw Aileen talking with Lucky over to the side.

"Well, the police are on the way. Y'all should be all set," said Lucky. "I gotta get moving."

Kurt wished him well, "Thank you for stopping, Lucky. You were great!"

Two police cars came along straight away, then an ambulance pulled up on the other side of the median. The paramedics made sure all of us were ok. The Police checked out the car. From certain angles, the car looked fine. But, when you looked at the side that we had slid on, it was all dented and smashed. The amazing thing was that the car had its same, solid basic shape. It really looked like you could drive away with it as is. The police assured us that wasn't true and called a tow truck.

"Aileen, this Volvo was amazing," I exclaimed. "We've got to get one of these."

While the tow truck was on its way, the EMTs from the ambulance came up to each of us. They gave us a quick check over, then asked if any of us needed to go to the hospital. When none of us needed care, they had us all sign releases to declare we were refusing care.

The tow truck arrived and collected the car. As they got ready to head to a nearby body shop, I wondered how the rest of us were going to follow.

"We can fit you in our squad car," said one of the officers. We climbed in and put our seat belts on right away.

The crazy thing was we were on the median, in the middle of an expressway. So, the officer took a look at his side view mirror on the right, saw an opening and hit the gas. We took off like a rocket, all pushed back hard into our seats. I reached my hand out and grabbed hold of the door handle. He used the median for a few hundred feet, but shot right into the fast lane of traffic. With his lights and siren blaring, he shot up to 90 mph in no time. We were only on the highway for 2 minutes before the officer shot off to the right lane to exit. After literally going through a near death experience in a car, to be zipping along at 90 mph, accelerating like mad, then dashing off to the exit was horribly unsettling. I looked over at Aileen and she gave me a look back like, "These guys are gonna kill us!" But she said nothing.

The police brought us to Frederico Body and Auto Repair in Palo Alto where the Volvo was being unloaded. Aileen and I sat in the lobby with Alex and James while Kurt and Diane got the rundown on their car.

"Kurt, tell Anthony and Aileen about our new plan," Diane said as they came into the lobby.

Kurt detailed the situation, point blank. "OK. So, the car is not being driven anywhere. They tell us it is likely totaled. So, Anthony and Aileen, you need to grab a bus back to Monterey. You have the keys to our Honda too, so you can pull that out of the garage when you go check in on the house. We are staying here tonight, in a hotel. We missed our flight and we just need a night to catch our breath."

"I've had a bad feeling about this flight for weeks," said Diane. "This accident was just the final straw. I think this is not the right time for the family to fly to England."

"So, we will be in touch tomorrow, Anthony, and let you and Aileen know the plan from there. But, for now, please take care of the house and pets for us. You are welcome to stay there tonight. Does that work?" Kurt asked.

"Yeah, whatever you guys need," Aileen spoke up first. I nodded along. "We are here to help and support."

"I'm just glad we are all safe and healthy," I said. Diane and Kurt pulled in for a group hug and we all smiled.

Aileen and I tracked down a bus from Palo Alto to Monterey. We had about an hour and a half before it left, so we decided to find a place to eat. We walked for about 10 minutes along the main street from the bus station, deciding sandwiches didn't sound good, or burgers, or Mexican.

"How about that Chinese place over there?" said Aileen.

"Sounds great, let's do it." I answered.

As we waited for our food, I had a question for Aileen. "What were you talking about with that Lucky guy?"

"Lucky was giving me a report on our accident." Aileen used air quotes with her fingers when she said "accident."

"A report?"

"Lucky is with the Agency. He was assigned to follow us to the airport today." Aileen said flatly.

"Assigned to follow us? You asked for surveillance. What for?" I was very confused.

"After that hiking incident, I started wondering a bit. I remembered you had told me that story about the picnic back when you first got to town. I was worried something more was going on."

"So, you had Agency staff looking out for me?" I said, clearly a bit offended.

"Just on out of the ordinary events like this, where someone could arrange for things to go wrong."

"Aileen, you really think someone is out to get me?" I was incredulous.

"No, Anthony, I don't think so." Aileen looked down and paused. "I know so. Lucky saw shots fired from the hills above 280, right before the car lost control."

"What? Shooting at Kurt's family?" I was shocked.

"When the Volvo got to Frederico's, I had Lucky work with the shop staff to check out that tire. He recovered a bullet, embedded in our rear right tire. The blow out tire." There were those air quotes again around "blow out."

It took me a minute to have this settle in. Our accident was not at all accidental. It was a well-designed event aimed at killing us.

"Why is someone trying to kill us?" I asked.

"It's not us, Anthony. It's you." Aileen gave me a concerned look.

My face sent back confusion as our food arrived.

"Anthony, think about it. You have had four near deadly accidents since last summer. No one has that many accidents happen in such a short time. I don't have any data on the other three, but I know what happened today was not an accident. There's a team trying to track down any evidence from the hillsides above 280 where our tire blew." Aileen was taking this situation very seriously as a team member at the Agency.

The hiking trip to Arroyo Seco - Aileen had saved me. The motorcycle trip up to Stanford - Doug had done his fancy riding on the motorcycle. The drive to Utah from Arvada - a few seconds further into the intersection and I would be dead. Now Kurt's driving to get us off the highway today. Four near death experiences indeed.

At the end of our meal, we got fortune cookies. I opened mine and ate the cookie as the fortune fell to my plate. Aileen picked up the fortune from my plate, read it, then showed it to me.

"Today will be your lucky day."

Chapter Twenty

AFTER THE DRIVE

Schelletz had failed three times. He went to ground after that, but the Oligarchs would find him in time. This was too important a job to leave in the hands of Schelletz - it was now in more capable hands, the hands of someone more accountable.

The new assassin had had to scramble to the hills above 280. He had staked out 101, expecting Johns to bring the family the way everyone drove up to the airport. Luckily, there was an outpost tracking Rogue, and they let the gunman know as soon as the car took the 280 exit.

But here he was, set up, with an even better view than he had managed for the 101. He could spot a car 5 miles south, track it closer and shoot from this hillside. He practiced it on 3 or 4 cars, tracking them for a mile or two as they got closer. Then, he'd point the rifle sight at the rear right tire and pull the trigger. With the gun unloaded, all that happened was a click.

He loaded the rifle and was ready for the car to come. Based on the report of them entering 280, they would arrive in the next 6 minutes. Using the rifle sight, he scouted every car coming up the highway, waiting for the dark blue Volvo to show up. Green Toyota. Red Ford. Blue Toyota. Black pickup. Yellow beetle. On and on.

Until, finally, the dark blue Volvo came along. He followed it for roughly a mile, keeping the sight on that rear tire, allowing it to get in range for a clean shot. The Volvo was humming along in the far left lane. If his rifle sight had been a speed gun, Professor Johns would be in for a pricey ticket. But, that's not why he was on the hillside today. He had a job to do. A job Schelletz couldn't handle - the fool.

He whispered the word "fool" as he pulled the trigger.

Immediately, the car jostled and did some small swerves. He watched as Johns struggled to move it off the road. He was headed toward the exit, then the inevitable fish tailing began. He headed for the embankment, glanced off it, rolled the car on its side, the Volvo held it's relative stability and slid across the lanes back into traffic. Just what he needed. Surely another car would come along and finish them off.

He saw a pickup pull over and slowly follow up the road as they slid. The pickup had a logo for a local body shop. The gunman put his attention back on the Volvo as the cars around it dodged the wagon, allowing the Volvo to thread the needle of traffic. Amazingly, the car made its way all the way to the median, bounced off the railing and came to a rest on its wheels.

What luck this Rogue had. Well, he was not going to get out of this one. The gunman was ready to go the next step and do it directly - no more hiding behind the accident concept. He lifted the scope to follow the folks inside the car. Then, out of nowhere he was blinded. He pulled back from the gun and there was no relief. That damned pickup - there was some sort of reflective device on it's side taking the sunlight and blanketing the hillside.

The killer couldn't make out anything along the road. He packed up the rifle and gear in 30 seconds flat. He checked the hillside for a route, then headed out in a dead sprint North from his position. He kept glancing down below and the reflection was still there. Suddenly, he came upon a fence between two properties. He threw the rifle case over the fence and onto the ground. He took three steps back, then in one swift move stepped forward, grabbed the top of the fence, and sprung over. He picked up the rifle case and started off North again.

He was about 1/2 a mile up the highway, and he was just about out of the range of the sun flare from the pickup. Then the sirens started. At first, he thought it was just in his head. Then, it got louder and had that Doppler effect so he could tell they were moving toward the accident.

He dropped to his belly and pulled out the rifle. His training as a sniper was coming in handy all these years later. Usually, he had people to do these things for him. But, he was enjoying the thrill of the chase, the adrenaline.

As he got the rifle together and pointed it down toward the accident site, he could just make out shapes. The sun flare was mostly effective in blocking his view, but he was just far enough to be able to make things out. Those were the kids there. Next he found the mom, Mrs. Johns, looking after the kids. There was

Rogue's companion talking to a guy in overalls - must be the pickup driver. It was tempting to pop these two Agency hacks, but that would alert Rogue to the ambush. They were small prizes compared to Rogue.

The sirens were louder and louder. Only seconds remained. There were two figures clustered together talking, clearly Johns and Rogue. They stepped far enough apart that the gunman could make out who was who even in this view with the overwhelming light. He zeroed in on Rogue and was ready for his shot.

At that moment, two squad cars pulled up, throwing off his sighting, and causing the whole group to scramble, come together, and prepare to talk to the officers.

Damn, shooting Rogue outright was a risk to begin with, more than he had intended to do. But, with the Police right there, he'd only have a 30% chance of outrunning them once he popped off the shot. Getting caught would do no good. Sure, Rogue might be gone, but that would put the whole operation at risk.

One more time, he pulled up the rifle, found the shape of Rogue walking along the median to approach the Agency woman. Sweat was dripping down the killer's brow. But, not a shake in his hands - that sniper training was robust, even down to his muscle control. Rogue was his, he just needed to twitch off two rapid shots. It would be the end of him. But, he needed all the muscle control he could muster to hold back and not pull that trigger.

"Damn!" He dropped the rifle to the ground, stood up, stomped up the hill a few steps, kicked at the ground and let out a wordless roar.

After two deep breaths, he walked back to the rifle, took it apart and put it in his case.

He would have to report back about the results of his efforts. He'd be calm, distanced, and analytical by that point. But for now, the failure was still stinging. He'd expected to end the day with that fiero sensation one gets after completing a challenging task. Like when you finish a battle with a boss in a video game, after 15 or 20 tries, you finally figure out the boss's weakness and take him down. He was ready to savor that moment in person, walk away knowing he'd been victorious and accomplished an important goal.

Instead, he was left with that fiery sense of one more failure. The goose got away once again.

Maybe Schelletz wasn't such a fool after all.

Chapter Twenty-one

BACK AT THE RANCH

Rancho Verde. That was the name of the housing development. Every town in California had a Rancho Verde. How could anyone tell them apart?

We unlocked the door to Johns' house after that long, exhausting day.

"Aileen, I'm tired of being lucky. I want to know what is happening. Who is after me?" I let my exasperation show.

"Anthony, if we knew, we'd tell you. This is the thing. The evidence of these attacks is nearly nonexistent. We've got some digging and analysis to do to work this out."

"Great. So, until we do, what am I? Bait?"

"No, Anthony, of course not. Every Agent is an invaluable asset. We go to all lengths to keep our own people safe. And you are an even more valuable asset to me." Aileen let herself get a bit personal.

It was tempting to fade into a bit of domestic life. Here we were in Prof. Johns' house, turning on lights, feeding animals, and all the bits of home life. So, I pulled her close, kissed her, and we went about these chores. But, the conversation was not over, just on hold.

After setting up our overnight bags in the guest room, I pulled out some ice cream and other ingredients to prepare some killer chocolate caramel shakes. I brought one to Aileen as we sat down in the living room.

"We've got to get us both out of here, on to new assignments," Aileen picked up the conversation thread.

"How does that help me stay safe?" I was not following how her plan worked yet.

"We can do two things. Set you up with a new identity. And, if I do the forward work, getting things established, I can make sure the environment is secure." Aileen had half of this organized already.

"So, what is our new assignment?" I hadn't felt like this assignment was truly complete yet, but I knew Aileen had the right idea.

"There are three being tossed around. Japan, Geneva, and Finland."

"But nothing settled yet, hmm…ok. Well, we'll get our act together soon," I said ponderously, and let the topic fade away.

The next morning, Prof. Johns called. "Here is the plan. I'm going ahead on my own to England. My dad's birthday is in a week. I want to be there for it."

"So, the family is going with you after all?" I asked.

"No, Diane convinced me that her instinct is right, she and the boys should not be traveling overseas right now. But, since we are in motion on a vacation, we want to take the boys somewhere. Her folks have a cabin in Oregon. We'll go up there for a week together. When I head off to England next week, she and the boys will stay on for a second week." Kurt laid this all out for me.

"So, you still need us for the original length of time? Got it. Not a problem." I was firm and reassuring.

"We really appreciate it. And again, I'm so sorry for that scary event yesterday on the 280." Kurt was deeply genuine in the concern he expressed.

"Please don't worry about it. It's not like you planned to have a blowout."

Kurt got quite serious and somber for a moment. "But, had I been doing the proper maintenance on the car, I would've gotten that tire repaired long ago. I took your lives in my hands and I failed you and Aileen."

"Kurt, I appreciate your concern. We both do really. But, there is no way we blame you for what happened. You performed well under the pressure of losing a tire at such speeds. Believe me on this, the blowout was definitely not your fault." I smiled at Aileen on that last sentence.

"Well, thank you. For your help at the house, and for understanding about the accident. We will always have this event to bind us together, eh?" Kurt was already a good friend, more than an instructor to me and Aileen.

"Yep, now get back to your vacation! Give our best to Diane and the boys. Don't worry about a thing down here." I said, getting back to taking care of the house.

Aileen also learned of our new assignment that morning.

"Well, it is coming together. I am off to Japan in three days," she said brightly.

"What? How about our commitment to Prof. Johns. I just told him we would take care of the house for two weeks." I didn't want to be apart from her so soon.

"Anthony, you are staying put, for now at least. Remember, I am the forward person. You won't follow behind for a month. You need to help get the Navajo team settled into their new work. A month is just about right for that." Aileen continued to be on top of the plan details.

We spent as much of those three days together as we could. The days were full of Monterey highlights. We went to the Farmer's

Market, ate snacks from the vendors, brought home great, affordable produce, and cooked an awesome meal together. We drove to Carmel, walked along the quaint shopping streets, bought some British candy, and had brie and a baguette on Carmel Beach. On her last day, we biked along the coast to Asilomar Beach, walked along the sand, explored the tide pools, and kissed on a blanket as we listened to the bagpiper down the way at Pebble Beach. Then we headed back to the Johns house.

"I have to be honest that this threat on my life has me worried," I said as we settled in at the house.

"Oh, you will be safe. There is quite a team keeping an eye out for you. I would be shocked if anyone could take another swipe at you right now." Aileen expressed great confidence in this news.

"What do you mean about a team? Wait, I think I don't want to know, Aileen. I have a feeling I'd be weirded out by the details." I was grateful more than anything.

She looked at me with deep affection in her eyes.

"But, Aileen, you are my protector. The one keeping me safe from harm. You will be 5000 miles away." Again, I was hesitant to see her leave so soon.

"That's why our best people are on this team. If I can't be here, I wanted to be sure the best were on the case. I am still looking out for you, Anthony." Aileen's eyes were filled with warmth.

"So, who is after me anyway. And why?" I was speaking as an Agent, wanting to understand the threat.

"Our analysts in DC can't pull together anything to work with. There just is not enough data. And I wish I could tell you why. That would help us identify who as well." Aileen was clearly concerned by the incomplete analysis to date.

Our final night together seemed to last forever. I held her in my arms and we talked for hours. We woke up the next morning ready for the next challenge in front of us.

"Aileen, I love you. You will do great in Tokyo. I can't wait to meet up with you there and get briefed on our mission." I let my deep love for her show through beyond the working relationship.

"I love you too, Anthony. Take care of yourself. I need you to help finish planning that wedding of ours." With that, Aileen climbed into a black SUV with nondescript government plates and was driven off.

Later that day, I made my way to campus and into the lab to get my mind off of this transition, of Aileen leaving. The Navajo team was digging back into Syria. After some saber rattling about the weapons attack, a diplomatic breakthrough happened. The Syria regime agreed to give up and dismantle its chemical weapons stockpile. While this meant war had been averted, there was a new pressure put on our analysis team. We needed to be able to verify the information forwarded by the Syrians. If they arranged to show the inspectors a certain set of facilities, we should be able to confirm what the inspectors were being shown, it's relevance to disarmament, and whether they were not disclosing some new or alternative facilities. There would be attempts to game the system, no doubt there.

This turned into a new layer of high stakes work for our analysts. They began with the list of declared sites. Using the Center for Nonproliferation Studies data plus DLI transcripts from listening posts, they worked to establish that these were real sites and not a smoke screen. Some in DC and in the Mid-East feared we were handed a bunch of high school labs to visit instead of real weapons facilities. Each day, the team would tick a few more sites off the initial list and clear the International Atomic Energy Agency teams to go in and check out the conditions. A few sites listed had come up as wild goose chases, but by and large the Syrians were being transparent. And fortunately, our team was able to help sift through the mess supplied in a hurry by the regime.

In addition, there was a parallel effort going on to hunt for undisclosed sites. DC analysts in the Department of Energy started this process. They looked at various data sets from past inspections, satellite monitoring, defectors providing program details, and similar sources. When they found suspicious sites, they would send a list to our Monterey program. The next day, the analysts would shift their efforts and try to determine what might be hidden or what was innocuous. This type of shift came every 5 or 6 days. It was a harder question because in a way you were trying to prove nothing was there. Or rather disprove that nothing was there. A slippery question.

Before I knew it, time moved along and Aileen had been in Japan for a week. She kept me updated and things were shaping up well. She couldn't share details yet, but she was confident I would be pleased with the next phase of work for the Agency...and life with her. I couldn't wait.

But, waiting is exactly what I needed to do. So, I stepped in to help the Navajo team address a set of the unannounced, but suspected sites sent to them from DC.

Alice told me, "I have a rhythm I use for these sites. First, I analyze connections between the new sites. Then, I look for connections between the new sites and all the other suspected unannounced sites thus far."

"Are you seeing anything with these first two comparisons?" I asked. Following along with the process Alice described.

"So far nothing. None of these cross with the other suspicious sites," Alice explained. "So, then I move in and look for connections with the known sites. This is usually more fruitful. Actually, this is typically how they got on our list to begin with. But, by using the 1000 Words system, I'm able to identify how they are related, to read documents that link them together. Sometimes a scientist has been at both facilities, sometimes there are government documents that discuss both sites, sometimes they are just in the same neighborhood with each other."

"So, what does a positive hit like this one here tell you?" I kept her moving through her process.

"This gives me a sense of the most likely connections. Once I've done this, I have a priority list for how to start digging through the list we were given," Alice was on a roll. "I start with the most likely ones given their relationship to known weapons sites. Then, I dig into themes related to each of the suspicious sites. I dig into just that site, not related to any other site. I gather up all the data I can about it and go to town with my typical theme-based discovery."

"So, what you just walked me through is only the beginning?" I was surprised by the complexity of the detailed work.

"Yep, Anthony. I've got a long day ahead of me," Alice was exasperated. "As important as these suspected sites are, I have to say the analysis is a bit annoying. We have never confirmed any of the suspicions from other teams. Maybe their filter for suspicion is really low, too low? Maybe they are totally out of whack with where their suspicions spring from. All I know is these are long days of pounding my head against a wall, with little or no reward of finding something to care about, or a site to investigate and maybe close down."

"This work is so important to making Syria accountable for their programs and their willful ignoring of world consensus on chemical weapons. I know it is hard," I said to Alice. "I know we are working you on really long days. But, your analysis has been so key to supporting this breakthrough. Finding no reason to suspect these sights is actually the best outcome, right? If you did find a hidden site, it would mean Damascus had been lying to us, undermining our trust that their plan to disarm is genuine. Get in there and get it done!"

When I knocked on the door to Earl's analysis room, I also said quietly, "Hello!?"

"Come in, Anthony. Here to take over for me?" Earl smiled.

"No thanks, Earl. You are so much better at this than I am. That's why you are part of this awesome team and I'm just sitting around watching you work." I walked into his room and sat down.

"Well, these are not my creative days, Anthony. When we have suspicious sites. I have to admit, the other 5 days of the week are more fun. I have my foolproof ten criteria for a weapons site. I analyzed all the real, confirmed sites and generated this profile that fits them 100% of the time. So, I just run all the criteria down on each site on the list. If they fail more than 3 of the 10, I can be confident they are not a real site," Earl was very matter of fact.

"So, do you drop them at that point?" I wanted to grasp his full process.

"No, I keep going so I can give them all scores out of 10. It provides a more thorough analysis to be sure I'm not missing something, but also gives me some data." Earl got a bit excited here. "There may be a chance to pull all the score data together after we are done with the Syria work and come up with some lessons learned about identifying suspicious sites."

"Great thinking. Thanks for the proactive approach." He nodded back a silent, "You're welcome!"

"So, Earl, as you walk through this second site, I see some overlapping characteristics from the first one. I assume you bundle up the suspicious sites to analyze against the 10 criteria, right?" I was eager to understand more.

"Actually, no. I've been sticking to individual analyses. Do you think it's safe to analyze clusters at once?" Earl liked this debrief on his process.

"Absolutely! That's part of the power of 1000 Words." I got excited and walked around a bit. "Take these 5 suspected sites. They are all in the same suburb of Damascus. If you test them all against the 3 locational criteria, you can see how they cluster by answer, and you get your individual yes or no flag on the specific criterion."

"Let me try that..." Earl said absently as he stood up and started working the new list of suspected sites. He was off and running, tearing through the list. I let myself out.

It was time for some fresh air and a cup of coffee. As I made my way to the door, Jason came up behind me. "Hey, Anthony!" He said.

We ended up walking to the cafe together. I picked up his coffee for him.

"Mr. Rogue, having you around the lab is always a help!" Jason seemed pleased to have me around.

"Thanks, Jason. But, I have to tell you something. My work here with you all is winding down." This was my first chance to share about the change.

He gave me a worried and puzzled look.

"I've got a new assignment shaping up. I am needed elsewhere." I smiled to be reassuring.

"Then what are we going to do?" asked Jason.

"Keep plugging away. You guys don't need me. I've done all I can for you guys." Again I kept a reassuring expression.

"Mr. Rogue," Jason grabbed my hand for a firm shake. "I want to thank you. You don't know how grateful I am. This work feels right to me. I feel like I was born to do this. I didn't know it at the time, but I didn't really fit in on the reservation. There was no work that bridged all these talents for me."

I let him keep going as we drank our coffees and walked through town. I was going to miss the sea air and noises of Monterey, so soothing and relaxing.

Jason continued, "I feel so alive inside the 1000 Words system. It feels like home. I sometimes pull up some visuals to make it look like Monument Valley. I admit I miss the scenery, and of course my family. But, this work, these tools, this experience is well worth the small sacrifices. If you are leaving soon, I just need you to know how much I appreciate this."

"Jason, you are so very welcome. You need not thank me. I was literally just doing my job. And now, the work you are doing is so important to the Agency and the country - that is all the thanks I need - to see you tracking these puzzles."

We both paused and kept walking.

"So, Jason, how is the suspicious site analysis coming?" I asked.

"Great. I'm all done. I found one site that needs to be looked at," Jason said proudly. "If I was a betting man, I'd bet on this one being a weapons site. It appears to be small, but large enough to hold some nasty work."

"Wow. How confident are you?"

"98%," he said. "Not based on any statistical analysis - just saying that's how strong I feel about my personal interpretation of the data."

"How do you process these suspected sites?" I kept digging.

"I cluster them. I find all the commonalities they have between them. I combine all the documents, data, photos, etc. that we have for each site. Then I put them into affinity groups, until they are all accounted for," Jason paused. "Next, I start crossing those clusters against known, documented weapons sites in Syria and other countries in the region. I can start eliminating clusters which don't provide such a clear picture of weapons work like the real sites do."

"And how did that lead you to finding the one site tonight that you speculate is a genuine weapons site?" I waned to confirm his confidence.

"Well, it stood out right away. It simply didn't cluster with the other suspicious sites. I couldn't connect it with any of them. So, then I started eliminating each of the clusters. Crossing them off, one by one."

"Until you had just the one outlier left?" I said.

"Yep," Jason said plainly.

"But you didn't just assume that meant it was a site, did you?"

"No, Anthony, come on. I'm not that simple minded. But, it was the only one left - everything else had quickly failed and fallen away. So, I could focus all my attention on this one remaining site. Then I just kept digging on it, deeper and deeper, focused, dogged. If there was a shred of data indicating something, I was going to find it."

"And you did!" I exclaimed.

"Yeah. This spot in the southeast of the country. Pretty isolated, but main roads make most of the trip easy to do."

"Ok, we'll see what they find," I said with an air of tasing in my voice.

At this point, we made our way back to the lab. Jason submitted his findings for the report back to DC, and he and I stayed awhile for a cold drink and to talk about the work he did with 1000 Words.

Another day with my focus not stuck on Japan and how Aileen was doing. Doing the work we had been here in Monterey to do. Soon it would be time to say goodbye, or farewell at least, to this place and this team.

THE BIG ASK

It was Sunday morning. I called Jason at 6 am.

"Hello?" He was clearly groggy. I had woken him up. But, I knew I was going to wake him up.

"Jason, hello. Anthony here. I am so sorry for waking you up. There's something important. Can I meet you at the lab in 20 minutes? I'll bring coffee and some donuts."

"Ok, Anthony. No problem." Jason was snapping up and coming to life already. A good man!

When Jason arrived, I handed him his favorite coffee and offered him a box of the best donuts in town.

"Healthier food is on the way later today, but these will have to do for now. Thanks for coming!" I was genuinely grateful.

"Where are the others? I didn't see them on my way." Jason was looking around.

"They are not coming. Jason, this is just for you. After I describe it, you have every right to walk away. And you can still keep the donuts." I smiled, trying to lighten the mood, before asking my big question.

"Jason, with that one suspicious site the other day, the other two analysts didn't catch it, but you were absolutely right. That's three times this month you have caught an unannounced site that the others missed." I paused for him to take this in.

"Wow. Ok. I'm glad it worked out." Jason remained modest.

"Yeah, even though we could only give them 15% certainty with one match from you three, they went ahead and pursued a site visit. And they turned up chemical weapons. Good work!" I wanted him to understand the value of his analysis.

"I'm sure you didn't wake me up, just to give me some good news and reinforcement," Jason said, then took a bite of donut.

I laughed. "Of course not. I've got a new analysis for you, just you. Off the books. It's not related to the Syria situation."

"I figured as much on a Sunday morning. Ok, Anthony, just ask me already."

"This one is personal, Jason. A favor, I guess... You see, someone has been trying to kill me." I looked him straight in the eye. Then I kept going. "Four times in the last year, I've been involved in near fatal accidents. The last one was definitely not an accident. We think the other three weren't either. But, no one can confirm this."

"Wow, Anthony. Who would want you dead?" Jason had a lot to learn about our work life.

"Excellent question. That's why I need your help." I paused for effect. "We don't know who is doing it or how this is being done. Or why, for that matter. But, I have some data sets that might hold the answer."

"Which is where I come in." A broad smile filled Jason's face, lit up his eyes. I could see his analytical process kicking in as he took off the fleece jacket he'd worn over to the lab.

"Jason, before you dive in. I can see how much you want to dive in. I need to say this clearly and directly. No one has authorized this work. You and I could both be disciplined or thrown out for doing this. If you do not want to take this on, I will not blame you at all. If there is fallout, I will take the fall and try to shield you. But, I can not guarantee any real protection." This was my best effort at giving him a clear, no guilt, out, before deciding to help me.

"Anthony, I understand. Now, get out of my way. We are doing this."

I showed Jason the data set I'd been able to cobble together. There were cell records of calls made from the towers near where each accident had been, documents about my past cases, information about this project, travel records in and out of the areas where the accidents occurred, police records and news clippings of reported incidents around the neighborhoods where these things took place. Really, it was a tangled mess of loose threads and random scribblings. Nothing as robust as what Jason normally had. But, he had ideas and approaches to try. So, I got out of his way.

I took a walk around downtown, refilling my coffee, thinking about this crazy situation. Then my cell rang. Did Jason already have something? No, it was a call from Japan - Aileen?

"Hello!" I said excitedly.

"Hi, sweetie." Aileen's voice was a salve.

"Aileen. Is this safe?" I started to get concerned.

"Yes, it's fine. This call can't be traced between us. Ha ha...We have ways." Aileen said the last line in a low, mock devious voice.

"It is so great to hear your voice, Aileen. You don't know. This has been a hard few weeks." I let myself relax in her presence.

"For me too. But, this is all coming together. This will be alright. Hang in there. How are the analysts?" Aileen shared her concern for the team.

"They have settled in and are working hard, whatever we throw at them, they dive in and tackle it."

"I am hearing great things about their Syria work," Aileen said with pride.

"I will give them your compliments. I'm sure they would want me to send them your best too," I said this knowing I couldn't really tell them about the call.

"An Agent will be in touch with you soon about the transition process, getting you into your new identity and on your way here. Keep an eye out for that," Aileen said as boss, not fiancée.

"You bet. I know it means we'll be together soon. Take care of yourself out there," I let the last idea linger.

"No, you take care of yourself. I love you."

"I love you too, Aileen." And with that the line closed as she hung up on me.

I came back to the lab and checked in with Jason, making sure he had access to all the data he needed. Then, I grabbed my bike and went for a ride. Talking to Aileen reminded me of the bike rides she and I would take. So, I followed that path. Through campus toward the water front, but still up along the hillside where campus was situated. Then, I rode down across Portola Plaza and toward Fisherman's Wharf. I rode along the water and looked up at the Presidio, gated-off, where the DLI is based. Here, I got into the bustle of Cannery Row, passing behind shops and restaurants, hearing people having a fun afternoon with family. Aileen and I would often slow down a bit here, ride side by side and hold hands for short stretches. As I passed out of Cannery Row, right along the water I looked out on the beautiful Monterey Bay Aquarium.

From here, the path broadens with the open water of Monterey bay on the right and houses up the hillside on the left. This part of the bay includes a few beaches where sea lions like to congregate and lie in the sun. It quickly gives way to Lover's Point, a beach that's interrupted by a rocky point jutting into the water. There are always scuba divers on the beach coming or going, maybe a few kayaks tooling around in this relatively calm portion of the bay. This is also the stretch where famous Victorian B&Bs line the roadway, affording great views of the water out across to Santa Cruz in the north.

The next stretch of the ride loses the path, with just a section along the road for bikes. Aileen and I would help each other look out for people in parked cars. When we saw someone readying to open their door, we'd call out "lunchmeat" as our code word. I called a few "lunchmeats" during my solo bike ride as a tribute to my exercise buddy, who was across the Pacific Ocean.

The Pacific - this ride was leading me to the Pacific. I passed a number of nice homes, a mixture of Victorian, mid-century, and newer construction. I passed a local golf course, turning the corner of the bay to see the truly wide open Pacific Ocean. I reached out a hand and waved to the West, across the Pacific to Aileen, quietly saying her name, "Aileen." Doing this made me self conscious of the Agency guard likely following behind me, to keep me safe in these weeks before going underground and becoming deeply safe.

Remembering this made me angry, frustrated at the limitations on my life and my work, disturbed that some group was trying to have me killed, worried that Aileen, even with Agency training and staff keeping her safe, was at risk because of these madmen. I picked up the pace of my biking to get off some of my steam. This part of the ride also opened up as most bikers turned back before this area. The neighborhood got more sparse with more space between the homes that looked out on the Pacific. The homes got bigger, nicer, looked more like one-off architect designs. This would be a place to own a home in Monterey, fairly peaceful and remote, yet not far from restaurants and shops in Pacific Grove.

The road continues along the Pacific for a mile or so, then turns inland. But before turning inland, it runs along Asilomar State Beach. This became our spot to commune with the ocean. Aileen had been here for bonfires with friends before I arrived. Once she shared it with me, it became a special place for us. Coming here made me feel close to her. I locked up my bike and went for a walk along the water. While I walked, I spoke with her - told her about the work from the Navajo analysts. Told her about my fears of these folks tracking me down, hurting her. Told her about how I envisioned living my life with her.

At that point, Jason sent me a text message. He had something for me. It was time to return to the lab and see what we knew from our data. I hopped on my bike and took the quick way back. Up the hill into downtown Pacific Grove, cutting down to the water in New Monterey, joining the path along Cannery Row, zipping past the Presidio, then back up through downtown to the lab. I was arriving about 8 minutes after the text message arrived, a bit out of breath.

"Ok, what do you have?" I asked nearly before I walked through the door.

"Anthony, this will take a bit to explain. Can we grab a bite?" Jason was already putting his coat on.

"Absolutely, Jason, it's on me. Let's get something tasty and talk this through. How about Thai?" I asked. So, we headed a few blocks away to a Thai restaurant with a great noodle dish with basil called Pad Kee Mao.

"So, it took some digging, but I have a pretty solid theory," Jason started in. "I was able to create a solid trail of data. First, I found intelligence reports that a well known assassin for hire had gone missing in the past few months. His name is Schelletz. The reports indicated that he likely was in hiding, because there was no indication he had been killed. The speculation was that he had botched a job.

"So, I dug into Schelletz a bit, found some of his known aliases in the FBI databases, and looked for any traffic of his. It was a bit of an early gold mine. I found evidence that put him in town for your first three incidents - Denver in the summer when you had the car accident, San Jose later that summer when you headed up for the picnic, then Carmel when you had the hiking accident. Here is the paperwork documenting his locations."

"Ok, so this is our guy. Where do I find him?" I jumped in, eager to bring some closure here.

"Well, as I said, he totally disappears at this point. No sign of him in months, anywhere in the US, anywhere in the world. No credit card activity, no cash movement, no plane or train tickets. And absolutely nothing connecting him to the car tire, the one incident where we have physical evidence that it was a purposeful affair."

"I don't understand," I said, a bit deflated.

"So, I had to back up. I put in a three strikes theory," Jason said, raising his eyebrows as he raised his voice a bit. "Remember, Schelletz is a gun for hire. He likely has no direct beef with you, he's just being paid to do a job. When he doesn't get it done on the third try, this drove him underground, to get away from whoever hired him. That's one avenue we could go down - to track him down and talk to him - but it's long and laborious - uncovering his trail takes more than a database jockey."

"But, you said you have something for me?" I was confused.

"Patience, Anthony, I'm getting there."

"Ha. Yeah, sorry. Ok, so where did you go next?" I turned back to my analyst mindset.

"My theory is Schelletz was hired by someone else. So, I needed to find links from him to someone else." Jason paused as he leaned in. "I tracked down what I could of his communication and travel that might have a pattern. You provided cell phone logs from the towers around the locations where you had your accidents. There was no phone that was in all three places. But, there were calls, or attempted calls made a few minutes after the accidents all coming from the same phone line. A San Francisco number. That seemed like too much of a coincidence."

"Wait, so Schelletz didn't show up at the same number in the neighborhood of each event. Maybe he had a different phone each time, burner phones. But, the same number in San Francisco called somebody in the target area right after each accident?" I asked to lead him further.

"Yep, actually, after the crash in Arvada, the San Francisco number was dialed from a cell phone on the same street as you. Then, in Santa Cruz, the same San Francisco number called a cell about 3 minutes after you sped away from the accident. Finally, the San Francisco number called but never connected to a cell phone that was originally located near the river bed where you all hiked and swam." Jason was thorough in his narrative. "Interestingly, the SF number tried the cell twice and no answer. And the tower records show the Arroyo Seco cell that was being called dropped off the network that afternoon - never picked up again by any tower anywhere, to this day."

"So, that San Francisco number is suspicious, but not much to go on there." I had jumped to a conclusion ahead of Jason.

"Well, I went back and strengthened the connection. I found other conversations between the San Francisco number and these three cells. They were all within a few days of your accidents. So, these were not misdials by 'Mr. Frisco.' I even have evidence of Mr. Frisco's number being at the same cell tower with the first of these three numbers, about a month before the Arvada accident - like an initial in-person meeting happened. In the Denver area, as well," Jason delivered these details with pride in his voice.

"I see a picture forming," I slowly uttered.

"Anthony, I could go deeper into the details. I have all night, if you really want to. But, let me just say that I've tracked down interaction between Schelletz, a known gun for hire and this Mr. Frisco. It all ties into your accidents. And I'm convinced Schelletz was the one trying to kill you at the start." Jason spoke confidently.

"No need to dig deeper. I get that Frisco hired Schelletz. So the $64,000 question is, Who is Mr Frisco?" I was ready to act.

Jason smiled and took a bite of his fried rice.

"Well, using the cell number for Mr. Frisco, I could track down who was paying for it. But to confirm I had the right person, the right Mr. Frisco, I wanted more than a few coincidental phone calls." Jason returned to narrative mode. "I had to go back to the final incident, shooting out the car tire on 280. I figured whoever did that, whether Schelletz under a different name, or someone entirely new, Frisco would be in contact with the gun for hire. Back to the cell tower records, and I had a hit - a connection with the same San Francisco cell number. But, get this, Mr. Frisco didn't call or talk to our shooter that afternoon."

"Frisco was on the hill himself. He was the shooter for accident number four, right?" I asked eagerly, a smile on my face.

"You got it, Anthony. You know guys like this. If their hired gun can't do it for them, time to step in themselves and get the job done." Jason had read too many spy novels.

"Wow! Ok, tell me about Frisco. Who are we dealing with?" I swung back into action mode.

"The name is George Dylan. He's a West Coast financial power broker. Made and lost millions, but mostly made them, riding the various tech expansions and bubbles in Silicon Valley. A private type. Shows up in the financial press for reasons of business headlines and highlights. But, little personal information or background available on him. I can't work out a theory for why he wants you dead." Jason seemed mildly frustrated, then said, "But, I've got plenty of evidence that he worked with Schelletz, and on his own, to take you out."

"So, how do I find this guy?"

"What are you going to do, Anthony? You're not going to..." Jason trailed off.

"What? Kill him? What if I was, Jason. Don't be such a prude. This is no game - when your life is on the line, this is very real. But, no, I am not going to kill him. I am dying to talk to the man, find out why he is after me." I delivered all this with firm Agency training behind it.

"Ok, Anthony. Thanks for the reassurance He's got two homes to check out. One is in San Francisco. The other is Park City, Utah. I have no idea which one he is at. Here are the details." Jason forwarded me the addresses from his phone."

I checked them out and started putting a plan together for tracking down Dylan for a chat. I snapped out of it and realized I'd gotten lost in my thoughts. I took a bite of my Kee Mao and looked over at Jason.

"Jason, you look like you have something more to tell me," I said before chewing the bite of dinner.

Jason paused. "What? Something more...Well...uh. No. No, nothing more."

"Ok. Well, I've got work to do. Thanks, Jason. Thank you so much!"

We finished our meals and I drove Jason back to the DLI. I definitely had work to do.

Chapter Twenty-three

PARK CITY

Jason had found George Dylan for me. Time to put this to bed.

But Dylan had two homes - no telling which he was in. Visiting one house before the other might tip him off and I couldn't be in two places at once. So, I made a call.

"Bill, hello! Anthony here."

"Anthony, wow! Good to hear from you. How are those kids doing in the Navajo project? We're gearing up for next summer to train in some more young ones," Bill explained excitedly.

"Alice, Earl, and Jason are doing great. The work they can do with the skills we surfaced in them has been incredible. Thanks again for partnering on that work!" I really wanted Bill to understand the importance of his work.

"Look, it was my dad's passion, and van Gotsche's concept really knocked us all out. We're so glad it is working out!"

"Hey. Bill, I need a big favor." I smiled as I said this.

"Um, ok, Anthony. Tell me about it," Bill muttered hesitantly.

"First, I have to warn you this is not official Agency business. It's off the books. More of a personal issue," I said in a soft tone.

"Anthony, I'm here for you." Bill was firm and clear.

"Again, if you don't like the sound of this, say the word and I'll back away. So, what are you, like 30 minutes from Park City?" I asked.

"Yeah, more or less," said Bill.

"Can you hop in your car and head that way while we talk? I need you to check someone out for me."

"Gosh, right now? Um, ok! I'm putting my shoes on. What's this all about Anthony?" Bill asked, bemused and confused.

"I need you to pay a visit to a Mr. George Dylan. He's been literally trying to hunt me down for the past year," I shared a bit more eagerly than I should have.

"That's crazy, Anthony!"

"I know. He's got two homes - one in San Francisco and one in Park City," I reported to Bill. "I'm on my way to the San Francisco place, so I need help with the Park City one. I'll text you the address."

"Ok, Anthony. I'm in the car and driving now. So, what do you mean he is hunting you down?" Bill needed more context.

"Well, I had a bunch of accidents, near misses, in the last year. Remember that car accident before I came to Utah? I told you about it once I arrived. That was just the first one - and it turns out none of them were true accidents, they were attempts on my life." I gave Bill the rundown of each event and the theory about Schelletz and George Dylan.

"Hmm, sounds like some analysts have been digging through a mountain of data on this one?" Bill noted sarcastically.

"Well, I only bothered one of them. I didn't want to get them all in trouble for my little mission here," I confided in Bill.

"Only one? I was talking with Steve the other day and he said the success of the project was about getting 2 or 3 of the kids to triangulate and reach similar conclusions."

"Wait - Steve? So, you did recruit Steve into the fold, then?" I asked Bill.

"Yeah. The summer in Monument Valley was a bit of a test case. By the end of the summer, he knew something was up and was not at all surprised. It took him awhile to decide," Bill explained.

"Well, yeah, he's no super fan of the way our government operates," I said slowly.

"There's more there beneath the surface on that one, though, Anthony. He has high expectations, sure. But, he's a realist too. Anyway, yes, he is one of us now. So, what about the triangulation?"

"So, yes, in an ideal world, we triangulate. But, this is not ideal - this is about putting an end to Dylan's manhunt. So, there's some risk the conclusion we are working from is not definitive. In my gut, it feels like the right thing," I emphasized to show my confidence.

"Ok, well I'm arriving at the address you sent, Anthony. I'll put in my micro-earpiece and you can listen in as I approach," Bill whispered this last piece.

"Got it, Bill. Hey, I need you to keep Dylan alive. This is no vendetta, no revenge hunt. I want this guy off the streets AND in our hands so we can learn about him and whatever his motivation is."

"You bet, Anthony. I'll bring him back alive."

"Be safe. Don't do anything foolish. I'll be listening the whole time," I whispered to Bill.

In a well-trained voice that was quiet, but entirely clear, ill narrated his experience. "The house is mostly dark, with one light on downstairs and two upstairs. I'm walking to the door."

I heard the doorbell ring. Then silence while waiting for an answer at the door. He rang again after a minute or so. More waiting.

"Anthony, I see no signs of movement anywhere. Time to check things out on my own.

"I'm in the garage. One stall has a car, the other is empty. No one anywhere in the garage," Bill continued.

"Now I'm off to the back of the house. Absolutely no sign of people, dogs, or an alarm system. I'll jimmy my way into a window."

I heard sounds of creaking wood and a muddled pop, then the sliding noise of a window. "I'm in," said Bill in a loud whisper.

There was a lot of silence. In the background, I heard the sound of running. "Anthony, there is something moving about upstairs. I'm seeing nothing on the main floor. Need to check a few more doors, but I do think someone is upstairs. Why would they not answer the doorbell earlier?"

"Bill, be careful. We don't know how sophisticated this guy is. There may be some challenges once you reach that top floor," I warned.

"Got it! Heading upstairs now," Bill responded.

The silence seemed unending. He was taking the wise precaution of making no extraneous noise just to talk to me. I could hear his breathing, imagining he was walking up some stairs, gun out and at the ready. Again, I heard footsteps and creaks from a distance, definitely not coming from Bill himself. Who was it? Were they ready for Bill? Listening to Bill approach the way he was listening for them?

I heard a door open and Bill sweeping into it. "Clear." The quietest whisper came through.

Again, another door and sounds of Bill sweeping in. "Clear."

With each room he entered and cleared, I felt a sense of relief. But, also a sense of building concern as I realized that Bill was getting closer and closer to whatever was making those noises.

As he made his way through the upstairs, I was arriving at the San Francisco house. A few lights on, but no obvious signs of activity. We were effectively acting like one person in two places - good timing.

"Clear." Another one down.

Then, a long silence, a deep breath from Bill, sounds of a door and lots of scurrying. Bill's feet, the other feet, a jump and a roll. Bill grunting and then throwing himself up against a wall with a thud. A pause of silence, then...

"Huh, huh, huh." In rapid succession...laughter?

"Ah, ha, ha ha." Bill's voice grew louder and clearer. Definitely humor in his voice. He was laughing.

"Bill! What's up?" I used a loud whisper.

"Sorry, Anthony. All is fine here. All clear. No one around. Well, no people," Bill reassured.

"No...people?" I asked.

"Yeah, when I got into the last room, the one with the lights, the master bedroom, I could tell the footsteps were coming from inside. I was ready to confront whoever was here. I opened the door and rolled into a crouch to one side. Looking up, there was no one around, but I heard footsteps on the other side of the bed. So, I did a dive and roll to the other side of the bed, ending up behind a small, upholstered chair pointing toward the bed. No shots, no one jumping me. So, I peaked around the chair and saw it...a raccoon, wait no, it was a cat. A big, gray, furry, and weighty cat. It really looked like the size of a small raccoon, but without the striped tail and mask for a face. Just a cat, heavy enough to make creaking sounds on the floor boards, but definitely not a threat. He came over to me, rubbed up against my leg and made a loud purring noise.

"But, I was not totally done clearing the room," Bill continued. "There was a master bathroom in the corner behind the bed. So, I threw myself up against the wall, peering into the door, confirming the bathroom was clear. That was that thud at the end - might've bruised my shoulder on that one. The raccoon cat had thrown off my focus a bit and I let myself come down hard on that shoulder."

"Bill, great work! Man, thank you so much. I really needed that checked out tonight so I could be sure we had run Mr. Dylan out of his foxhole." I paused, then explained, "I'm at the San Francisco house now. I arrived while you were clearing the Park City place. I guess we know where Mr. Dylan is!"

"Anthony, be careful, friend. Are you ready for this? Why not call in some backup? The Agency wants to protect you - they will support you on this," Bill pleaded a bit on this last part.

"I'm afraid I'm too far down this path, Bill. This is personal. I need to address this on my own. I don't want to pull anyone else into my trouble here. I feel bad enough pulling you and my analyst partner into this, but especially you. I figured it was only a 20% chance he was there in Park City, but I am still really glad you came up empty handed," I said as my focus turned toward my next goal.

"Ha, ha, Anthony. But you are not on your own," Bill reassured me. "The Agency has already been right beside you. We always will be. Go take care of this thing!"

Chapter Twenty-four

MR. FRISCO

This was not an area of San Francisco I'd ever visited before. These were the fancy homes, in the hills overlooking the city and the bay beyond. This is definitely what you would call prime real estate.

As I drove through the neighborhood, listening to Bill complete his sweep of the Park City house, questions kept popping into my head. Who has this much money? What do they do for a living? Rob banks? Maybe, just maybe. It depends on how you define "rob" I suppose.

Unlike what Bill found in Park City, there were no signs of life upstairs in Dylan's San Francisco home. It was a big, beautiful modern style home. Stark white exterior, lots of huge windows facing the best views on the property, flat roof and sharp corners, very geometric, yet stylized. An architect had studied this property carefully and etched a structure that made the absolute most of the surroundings. The lowest level of the house was built partly into the hillside, so it emerged organically from the terrain. At once integrated into the environment, yet standing out and saying clearly that someone had taken up residence here. While large, in the end, it did not feel oversized or ostentatious. Just the right size to contain a family comfortably.

Whatever I could say about Dylan and his efforts to kill me, whatever feelings I had about this mystery man with a beef about me and my work for the Agency, I have to say I wanted his house. A beautiful place.

So, after sizing the place up, I needed to make a plan of approach. The upstairs was dark, but the front, most prominent section of the house was lit up, three or four rooms, like a living area, kitchen and surrounding rooms. Looking through the big windows, I saw a flickering blue light.

"Blue light!"

When Aileen and I walked through Monterey at night, we'd see the family rooms of families all around town lit up with the blue light. Television. "Blue light," we'd say to each other with sort of a zombie voice. We liked to make fun of the way so many people spent their evenings stuck in front of televisions sets. In our culture, TV sets are always getting bigger, making their way into more rooms like bedrooms and even kitchens, continuing to become more prominent in every aspect of life. We tried to stay out of the lure of the blue light in our lives, while admitting it was alluring, very alluring to two children of the 70s. From our vantage point of TV asceticism, we enjoyed making fun of the worship of the blue light in so many other homes.

Aileen. What would she think of this solo investigation I was on? I'm sure she'd be disappointed. Not surprised, probably. But, disappointed that I'd taken it on, on my own, outside of Agency protocols.

Under my breath I whispered, "Sorry, Aileen," then headed toward the house.

I wanted to come in where it was dark, and make my way down to the blue light last, where I was most certain to find George Dylan and whoever else might be with him this evening. I ran up the hillside and around back. There was an easy climb from the hillside that the house was built into, to what was a second story window on this property. I was able to quickly work open the lock and let myself in. I cleaned up the lock quickly so it would show no signs of force later, assuming I could find a better exit.

The room I'd entered was a guest bedroom. Perfect. Rarely used, unlikely to have people coming and going. I took a moment. Knowing Bill was done with the Park City house, I figured my chances of finding Dylan at home here were high. I was in no rush anymore, so I got down on my belly on the bedroom floor, put my ear to the ground, and listened. I heard my own heart beat, heard the blood rushing through veins in my ears, heard air moving through the house duct work, and I could hear voices. Soon, it became clear the voices were on the TV, voices of actors I recognized from an art house movie I'd seen with Aileen 3 months before.

After a few minutes, there was no change to the sounds in the house. Either no one was there, or they were all in the living room, focused on the movie, making only the sounds of breathing and soft conversation. Time to move forward through this place.

I remained 80% confident there was no one upstairs to contend with, but I needed to know for sure before heading down to that main floor. After clearing the closets and other parts of the room I was in, I moved quietly to the room next to it. Also clear. I didn't have anyone on the phone with me like Bill had had. No reason to whisper "Clear!" each time I'd finished a room. Yet, the temptation was there, so I kept track in my own head, silently calling out "Clear!" to myself.

I didn't want my upstairs survey to alert those downstairs to my movements, so I made it through the rooms as quickly as I could. Second guest room - clear. Hallway bathroom - clear. Office - clear. Master bedroom and bath - clear. On that last one, I kept my eyes open for raccoon cats to trip over. There were none, but I giggled inside a bit envisioning once again the sight of Bill making his way through the master bedroom and bath in Park City.

Time to make my way downstairs. I took a deep breath and crept along the stairs, down low, taking in as much of the scene as I could at each point. The stairs came down between the front entry and kitchen area all aglow with light and TV. I heard music coming from the kitchen as well as the movie in the living room. This was a particularly gripping part of the movie, so I was confident the watchers would be sucked in. Behind the stairs were some dark rooms, perhaps a bathroom and work room or other secondary space. Plus, I could see the door leading to the garage.

I took advantage of the movie action and quietly slipped into the dark back area. At each door, I paused to listen to what was behind the door, and at the same time I looked back at the living room to see if anyone was aware I was in the house. Behind the first door was the garage. I quietly swung the door behind me to hide from the living room and scout the garage at the same time. No one there, one car was parked, and the other side was empty - just like Park City.

Back in the house, I made my way to the other two rooms. I swept into the first and it was the bathroom I had envisioned. Again, no surprises, no one sitting on the stool to frighten with the gun in my right hand at my hip.

Finally, I swept into the last room, cleared it of any signs of life, and made my way back to the hallway. I crouched down at the corner leading into the kitchen. Once again, I listened for conversation or signs that I'd been found out. Nothing but the movie and kitchen music. After about thirty seconds, it was time to approach the kitchen. I rolled around the corner, coming up on one knee, gun ahead of me, pointed through the kitchen and toward the living room. No one, no action, no food or dishes out in the kitchen. Through the doorway between the kitchen and living room I could see the couch. No one turned to look at me. I paused and listened. Nothing.

There was only one place left to investigate. Only one place left where George Dylan could be. Seated somewhere in the living room, watching the movie.

I slipped through the kitchen and quietly threw myself up against the wall leading from the kitchen to the living room. Two deep breathes to calm down and listen, then action.

I jumped through the doorway, gun out in front of me, took a quick visual sweep to my left, then dove to the right, rolled and came out pointing right back at the large sectional couch.

No shots, no one jumping on top of me. A quick two seconds to take in my surroundings. The couch was empty. Empty! No George Dylan, no one at all. Not even a goddamn raccoon cat.

My heart was in my throat, adrenaline pumping. But, my training told me the house was totally clear.

On the side table, I spotted a touch screen remote for the entertainment system and picked it up.

Suddenly the blue light turned off. But, no one was around? Who had turned it off. I was holding the remote, so how was someone able to control it? Then, the music cut off a few seconds later. Finally, the lights in all the rooms but the kitchen dimmed and shut off. Finally, I saw a light pop on over on the stairway. Still, I could see or hear no one.

Either this house was haunted, or I was losing it. I looked around carefully, taking in the scene to see what else had changed, what clue there was to what was happening in this house? Was I in danger. Then, on the wall, in this new relative darkness, I saw it. It sort of appeared to be a smiling face - but not really - and it was at eye level, just inside the living room wall adjoining the kitchen. I walked closer and it came into focus.

"Living House Systems" the screen said along the bottom. Home automation. The TV, music and lights were all part of Dylan's home automation system. No one was home at all, no ghosts, just the ghost in the machine on the wall, controlling the house.

With a home automation system like this, there must also be some security in place as well. Sure enough, I could see some flashing lights on the hills below and could hear the sirens approaching the house. A quick panic hit - should I run for it? No, I had let my investigation run it's course and turned up empty handed. The Agency would need to know about this now. Plus, someone at the Agency had been keeping tabs on me the whole time, so they knew at this point. Ultimately, the police coming to the house were on the same side as me. I would simply show my identification and let them know I was with the Agency. In fact, I dialed 911 so the dispatcher could alert the officers that I was not a threat in the house, and they could enter peacefully.

This left the big question - where was Mr. Frisco? I still was no closer to understanding why he was after me.

Chapter Twenty-five

TAHOE

"Steve - Steve Shimizu. It's Jason here."

"Jason, wow. So good to hear from you. What's up?" Steve responded cautiously.

"I need your help. Discretely."

"Oh, ok. I'll do whatever I can to help you," Steve assured Jason. The two had connected in Monument Valley, and Steve had become an Agency resource who sometimes helped Jason in gathering data for 1000 Words requests.

"It's actually Anthony that needs help. But, he doesn't know I'm calling you."

"Anthony? What help does he need?" Steve uttered with confusion.

"Someone is trying to kill him. He's out right now tracking the killer down," Jason said haltingly.

"Wow. Crazy! And you need me to back him up. Where is he?" Steve was in motion, ready to respond.

"Actually, I need you in Tahoe - can you get there tonight?" Jason asked sheepishly. "I told Anthony about two places where he might find this guy, but there is a small chance he's in a third place in Tahoe. It seemed like a distraction to tell him about Tahoe. But, now I am feeling like it needs to be checked out. Can you do it?"

"Absolutely. I'll get headed there right away. But, you have to give me all you've got on this guy," Steve firmly but gently demanded.

"Of course. I'm sending you a secure email as we speak, but I'll give you the highlights while you travel," Jason said.

With that, Jason set in motion a third front in tracking George Dylan that I knew nothing about at the time. This is what I was able to put together talking to Steve and Jason the next day.

Jason caught Steve up on the back story and everything we knew about Dylan while Steve was on his way to Tahoe. The Tahoe address had very little strength in Jason's analysis. There was just a thin thread attaching Dylan to this place. So, Jason had held back in telling me about it. But, with Steve available to help, the hunt was still on.

Steve made his way to Tahoe and the address where Dylan might be. It was a simple cabin, compared to the other two places, two floors with just two bedrooms, about 2500 square feet. Steve spent a few minutes scoping out the place. Not only were there lights on, but Steve could see shadows of a man walking through the living room back and forth.

Steve's training was fresh, since he was new to the Agency. He knew how to case out a target like this, and how to quietly approach it for a better look. From behind a neighboring house, he looked for signs of activity inside. Was this one person alone moving back and forth, or a bunch of people inside? After a few minutes of watching, it was clear the target was alone. That made Steve feel better. He knew he was supposed to take Dylan alive. So, having him alone meant fewer threats to Steve, and less chance he'd need to pull out lethal force.

Looking around the cabin, the main thing Steve noticed was it backed up to a lake. Rather, the lake, Lake Tahoe. It was a gorgeous setting, and the cabin had broad views over the lake. This would be an excellent place to spend some downtime, you know, if you happened to have some extra money around for a place in the mountains.

Steve made his way to a side door to the garage. It was locked, but he didn't let that slow him down. From the pattern of the person inside the house, this seemed like the best angle to come in. Unsure whether Dylan would be expecting him, he wanted to scope out as much of the house as he could before confronting him.

Steve checked whether the door to the house from the garage was open. The knob turned when he tried it. He kept his gun tucked away, turned the knob all the way and quietly slipped inside the door.

When he looked up, he was staring directly at Dylan, who had a gun in his left hand, trained on Steve.

"Who the hell are you?" Dylan asked.

Steve paused before he spoke.

"I said who are you?" The voice was louder and more insistent, but not yelling.

"Steve. Steve Wehrmacht. I didn't think anyone was here. Please don't shoot me. I was just looking for jewels. I'm so sorry, please don't shoot me." Steve pretended to cower.

"Oh, don't play games with me! You are not after jewels. I was expecting Anthony Rogue to walk through this door... You're not Rogue? But, I know you are Agency. Right?"

Steve wasn't sure how to play this. The training had not gone through a scenario like this. Dylan had totally ambushed him. He was calm and analytical - the training had built those assets. Where was his advantage? For now, it was in being honest, truthful.

"Yes," Steve said. He knew to answer directly, but be precise and not offer more information than he needed to.

"Give me your gun!" Dylan waved his gun at Steve, showing agitation and anger.

Steve complied. He was reluctant, but in training, they discussed the psychology of moments like this. Your only hope was to bring the temperature level down. Only a genuine psychopath on the other side of this situation would not want to bring the temperature down. Nothing from Bill's profile of George Dylan indicated psychopathy. As he took the gun, Dylan laid it down on an end table next to him.

"So then, who are you?"

"Agent Steve Shimizu."

"Steve Shimizu? Ok, Steve, what are we gonna do now?" Dylan posed.

"I don't know. You tell me." Steve was trying to keep Dylan talking.

"I don't have any beef with you, or with the Agency, for that matter. It's just Rogue." Dylan seemed exasperated.

While Dylan spoke, Steve was taking a look around, getting acclimated to his surroundings. They were in a family room, with a wet bar just to his left. Behind Dylan was a doorway to a kitchen. Then, to the right was a large living room space - it had a sectional couch, some chairs, and a sliding glass window that opened up onto a deck overlooking the lake, with two large picture windows on either side of the door. It was essentially a wall of glass with views of the lake.

"Where is Rogue? Did he send you? He must have sent you."

Here, Steve could continue to be truthful, while not delivering any important information.

"Anthony Rogue did not send me. I don't know where he is. Last I heard, he was living in Monterey." Steve delivered all this clearly and succinctly.

"I know he's in Monterey. You think I don't know that? I know Anthony Rogue!" The anger appeared again. "He's not going to get away with this." Now, Dylan was starting to get a distracted look. Steve could tell his thoughts were turning to how to get Anthony. He had thought Rogue would be standing here, and now he needed to track down Rogue himself.

"I know he's trying to slip out of the country, become harder to find in a sea of 7 billion. Well, we have people and contacts everywhere. We'll find that lucky son of a gun. He took a bite out of the Oligarchs in Poland. He can't be allowed to take one of us down without repercussions."

Steve had never heard of the Oligarchs before. He knew Anthony had been in Poland after graduating from Caltech. But, he knew nothing about any missions or altercations there. Clearly something powerful had happened.

"So, you knew Anthony in Poland?" Steve was taking a risk. Asking questions could draw the attention back to him. But, he was hoping that thinking of Anthony in Poland would agitate Dylan again, get him off guard.

"What? Are you asking me questions? I ask the questions around here!" He focused in on Steve, bringing the gun back up a bit.

Steve decided that had been the wrong move. Sure it agitated him, but the focus did come back to Steve.

Just then, Dylan's phone buzzed. Only important messages would make it through his do not disturb settings. He kept an eye on Shimizu, but pulled it out of his pocket. It was a message from his security system in San Francisco, alerting him that someone was in his home. This must have been about the time I was making my way through that San Francisco house to the living room.

Steve saw this opportunity and took it. While Dylan looked down at his phone, he lunged to the left behind the wet bar. Dylan quickly recovered and shot at him. The bullet grazed Steve's shoulder as he disappeared behind the bar.

Before Dylan could recover and get another shot off, Steve grabbed a bottle of Zybrovka vodka and threw it over the bar. It hit Dylan on the side of the head, giving Steve an opening. He charged Dylan, knocking him down and throwing the gun across the floor.

Dylan was disarmed and disoriented from the blow to the head. But, he was not going down so easily. He kicked Steve off of him and rolled to the side. This was his turf, and he knew his best options. He tossed a side table at Steve, knocking him down. Then Dylan bolted for that sliding glass door.

When Steve stood up, Dylan had disappeared. Steve considered grabbing one of the guns, but knew he'd lose sight of Dylan if he paused. So, he launched himself toward that sliding glass door to go after Dylan. Steve was not going to let him get away.

He got to the deck, looking down toward the lake. Steve paused in a protected position. There were no gunshots, so Dylan must be disarmed. There was a small cluster of woods between the house and the lake. Steve pursued Dylan into the woods.

He could hear the rustling of a body moving quickly through the trees down toward the beach and he pushed on. When Steve reached the clearing of trees at the waters edge, he could see Dylan in the water, swimming. About 200 yards out was a small speed boat. There was no other boat around. If Dylan made it there, he was gone. This was why he took off, he knew it was a better chance than wrestling with an Agent around his house searching for weapons strewn about.

Steve ran a few steps into the lake, then launched himself into the water. The cold hit his entire body like an electric shock. But, he didn't have time to be cold. Steve had been a competitive swimmer in high school, so he tore off at great speed.

Steve closed the distance between him and Dylan pretty quickly, but it was unclear if Dylan would make it to the boat. As Dylan reached forward, about to grab the ladder and climb aboard, Steve grabbed his foot and pulled him back 12 inches.

Dylan kicked and released from his grip. He knew he'd have to take on Shimizu in the water before he could get into the boat and pull away.

The water was not deep. So, Steve pulled back and stood up with the water up to his chest.

Dylan grabbed the ladder and pulled himself partway up. He turned around and lunged at Steve, taking him underwater. Dylan had the initial advantage, holding Steve down for a good 35-40 seconds. But, they both were underwater as Steve struggled to get free.

Finally, Dylan had to back away to get a breath, and Steve squirmed off under the boat. He came back around the boat, used the ladder for leverage and launched himself at Dylan. He had a rock from the lake in his left hand. As he came down on Dylan, he slammed it into Dylan's shoulder.

The rock took Dylan by surprise, knocking him off his stance. "Aagh!" he called out in pain as he fell over. Steve was on top of him, standing above him, holding him underwater for a moment, getting a firm grip, establishing that he was in control. He let him up out of the water.

"This is over, I'm taking you in!" Steve exclaimed.

But Dylan was not ready to consider this finished.

"My life as George Dylan is over. Now that you guys have discovered me, there is no going back. That's what you've done to me! You are not taking me anywhere." With that, he grabbed Steve by the throat. For a billionaire oligarch, he was in amazing shape and incredibly strong. Steve felt the tightness increasing on his throat? He rolled Dylan underwater, got him to let go of his throat, then attacked a pressure point to knock him out.

Dylan finally stopped fighting, and Steve pulled his head above water. Steve's lifeguard training kicked in and he used a rescue hold to transport Dylan back to the beach.

As he brought him out of the water and laid him down, Steve was getting concerned. He leaned down, felt for a pulse, and found nothing. Dylan was not knocked out. He was dead. This was not easy for Steve. I had wanted Dylan brought in alive. Sure, Steve's own life was in danger from this desperate man. Dylan had shown how determined he was to kill me, and had made it clear he was willing to take out Steve to get away. But, Steve had never intended to kill Dylan. He thought he was just getting him under control in the water. Steve had never killed anyone. In time, he'd realize it was the only move he had left. But, at this moment he was shaking.

Steve went back inside to use a phone, called Jason and gave him the rundown. As I completed my work at the San Francisco house debriefing the police, I connected with Jason and he let me know what had happened. I took a deep breathe, the deepest one I'd taken in a long while. Then I called Steve to give him my personal thanks.

Chapter Twenty-six

THE RISING SUN

The plane landed at Narita airport in the dark.

Aileen had changed. I could see my beautiful Aileen inside, but she had changed. The picture in my head of how she looked had to be rapidly adjusted. Her face was thinner. Not gaunt or unhealthy, but less full than before. It would become clear that the lifestyle in Japan had shaved a few pounds off her frame overall. I'm sure I had changed too. A month apart can do that.

Aileen had already gotten mad at me when she heard what had happened with George Dylan. She was distressed. The Agency always preferred no loss of life on either side. In the debriefing, it became clear that Steve had done everything right. There was nothing he could have done differently without losing Dylan in the process. And, once we had confronted Dylan, if we didn't bring him in, he would have been more dangerous than before.

The Agency would need to work out who the Oligarchs were. This was not an organization we had on our radar. We had three homes worth of artifacts and data from Dylan to start our research, but the group was a genuine mystery.

Aileen was concerned that I'd brought Jason and Bill, and indirectly Steve into this mess. I had been irresponsible, especially given the genuine peril Steve was in. Any one of us could've been seriously hurt. And it was a real trial by fire for Steve.

She was irate that I'd taken it in my own hands to track down Dylan, that I'd used Agency resources to build the data set for Jason, and that I'd gone on one analyst's conclusions when I did act. Every step violating guidelines and important restrictions, showing a real disregard for the authority structure at the Agency. And risking my own life by aiming to directly confront someone who had repeatedly tried to kill me. That was her biggest concern. If things had gone awry, she would not just have lost a valuable Agent, she would have lost the love of her life.

But, that anger was all behind us from a week ago (or at least mostly behind us). Now, my plane had touched ground and we were reunited. We embraced for the longest time, saying nothing, then I spoke up.

"I love you." Three simple words.

"I love you, too," Aileen replied.

We held hands as we walked to baggage claim. We got my things and headed to a train into Tokyo. From the train window, I could see the sun rising over the sea. The blazing half circle was bursting to life, cleaning away the nightmares of the dark night that had just passed, alerting the animals and plants to wake up and start a new day.

"Aileen, this is a new day for us. A chance to start fresh. I absolutely can't wait!"

She smiled, kissed me, and pulled me tight.

Work would start up soon enough. I would tell her all about my days in Poland. Together we could figure out what harm I had done to anyone there, and who these Oligarchs might be. But, for now, I was safe in the knowledge that the Agency was working to protect me. I could confidently walk around as Anthony Rogue, the person I'd always been. The Agency had gathered a lot of intel about the Oligarchs and how they had targeted me. By removing Mr. Frisco, I had escaped this pattern of near misses.

And I was safe in the arms of Aileen.

We had a new culture to dive into and explore together in Japan. We had a new project to get off the ground for the Agency. And we had each other.